ABOUT THIS BOOK

THE WARRIOR GODDESS: ATHENA
Doris Gates

Athena, the warrior goddess, was born fully clothed and fully armed from the head of her father, the mighty Zeus. She was his favorite child and one of the most important of the gods, for she was goddess of wisdom and of the household as well. Her wrath could be as vengeful as that of her father, as those who crossed her discovered, but heroes were dear to her.

So here are the splendid tales of:

Perseus—who with Athena slew Medusa, the Gorgon
Andromeda—the lovely maiden rescued by Perseus
Pegasus—the wonderful winged horse
Jason and the Argonauts—who went in search of the
    Golden Fleece
Arachne—the boaster who was turned into a spider

DORIS GATES

The Warrior Goddess
ATHENA

Illustrated by Don Bolognese

Puffin Books

Penguin Books Ltd, Harmondsworth, Middlesex, England
Penguin Books, 625 Madison Avenue, New York, New York 10022, U.S.A.
Penguin Books Australia Ltd, Ringwood, Victoria, Australia
Penguin Books Canada Limited, 2801 John Street, Markham, Ontario, Canada L3R 1B4
Penguin Books (N.Z.) Ltd, 182-190 Wairau Road, Auckland 10, New Zealand

First published by The Viking Press 1972
Published in Puffin Books 1982

Library of Congress Cataloging in Publication Data
Gates, Doris, date. The warrior goddess: Athena.
   Originally published: New York: The Viking Press, 1972.
   Summary: Retells the Greek myths in which Athena plays a major role,
including those of Perseus, the Golden Fleece, and Arachne.
   1. Athena (Greek deity)—Juvenile literature.
[1. Athena (Greek deity)   2. Mythology, Greek]
I. Bolognese, Don, ill.   II. Title.
[BL820.M6G37 1982]   292'.211   82-7684   ISBN 0-14-031530-6   AACR2

Printed in the United States of America
by Offset Paperback Mfrs., Inc., Dallas, Pennsylvania

*These stories are all dedicated to
the boys and girls of
Fresno County, California,
who heard them first*

CONTENTS

The Warrior Goddess

The Birth
of Athena

She sprang from the head of Zeus, father of gods. Born
without a mother, she was fully grown and fully armed.
Her right hand gripped a spear, while her left steadied a
shield on her forearm. The awful aegis, a breast orna-
ment bordered with serpents, hung from her neck, and
from her helmeted head to her sandaled feet she was
cloaked in radiance, like the flash of weaponry. So the
great goddess Athena came to join the family of gods on
high Olympus, and, of all Zeus's children, she was his
favorite.

Her strange birth was in keeping with her role of
Warrior Goddess.

One day Zeus, sprawled upon a cloud floating above
Olympus, suddenly felt a pressure inside his skull. He
shook his head and passed his fist before his eyes. He

might have been brushing away a gnat. But the pain persisted and even increased. The pressure built up inside his head until at last he could no longer endure it in silence. His agonized bellowings thundered down the sides of the mighty mountain and shook the earth below. Men at work in the fields and meadows gazed upward fearfully, wondering what new calamity was in store for them. Mothers hustled their children into their little huts, threw more wood onto the smoky hearths, and waited for the storm to break.

Leaping down from his cloud, Zeus raged among the mansions on Olympus, seeking his son Hephaestus, god of the forge. The lame god came hobbling into sight as the other gods hastily assembled.

"Make haste," cried Zeus, "before this pain destroys me. Take your heaviest ax and split my skull."

Hephaestus stood aghast. Even though a god could not be killed, the command shocked him. Strike the father of gods! Split the skull of Zeus, mighty lord of the sky! It was unthinkable and the lame god stood hesitant and afraid.

"Fool," roared Zeus, "do as I command you or by the Styx I will hurl you from heaven as I did before, and this time you will not return merely lamed. I will fling you with such force that you will be lost forever in the limitless wastes of space."

Hephaestus limped off before the full threat had time to reach his ears. He had once before experienced his father's wrath and had a crippled leg to prove it. Now he hastened to his forge, and, glancing with an expert's eye over the tools arranged there, he chose his heaviest bronze ax and hurried back to where the suffering god awaited him.

Zeus knelt, and, as the others watched in stunned silence, Hephaestus brought the ax down upon the mighty skull. The sound of the impact was as when lightning strikes an ancient tree and splits it to its roots. A cry rose from the assembled gods. With a rattle of weaponry, a maiden, sternly beautiful, sprang forth from the huge skull. Thus was Athena born.

She was to become one of the most important of all the gods. She would be worshiped as the goddess of wisdom as well as of war. She would teach women the art of weaving and all other household crafts; they would call upon her during the pangs of childbirth. But though heroes would forever be dear to her, she would never know romantic love.

The first battle Athena took part in was a crucial one. Zeus, in order to become king of the gods, had had to overthrow the family of Titans. His own father, Cronus, was a Titan, as was Prometheus, who gave fire to man. Cronus was a monster who devoured his own children and would have done the same to Zeus at his birth except that he was tricked into swallowing a stone instead. As soon as he was grown, Zeus made war upon the family of Titans and vanquished them, thus establishing his reign on Mount Olympus.

But still there remained a horde of giants, the Gigantes,

who resented Zeus and determined to be rid of him. They were hideous creatures with scaly bodies and the tails of dragons. One had a hundred arms, and another was so huge he covered nine acres when standing.

The giants emerged from the Underworld in a place in Thessaly called Phlegra, across the sea from Mount Olympus. Just south of the sacred mountain is Mount Ossa, and some distance south of that is Mount Pelion. The giants knew that the only way they could conquer the gods was to fight them on their home ground, Mount Olympus. In order to do this, they waded across the deep waters that lie between Phlegra and Mount Pelion. Arriving at the base of the mountain, they reached down and plucked it up from the plain and carried it northward to Mount Ossa. There they piled Pelion on Ossa, thus forming a stairway to the summit of Olympus.

The giants fought with savage fury, and the victory might have been theirs if it had not been for the wisdom and warlike daring of the warrior goddess Athena. She was everywhere upon the field of battle, guiding her chariot fearlessly to where the fighting was heaviest. Early in the war, she had counseled Zeus to send for Heracles to help them, for in her wisdom Athena knew that the leader of the giants could be finally overcome only by the blows of a mortal. A son of Zeus, Heracles was born of a mortal mother and was second only to the gods in strength, and he gladly answered the summons of the father of gods. He attacked Alcyoneus, leader of the giants, and was astonished to discover that the giant was able to endure his

blows and even to fight back strongly. No one before had ever received a blow from Heracles and lived! Athena, quickly realizing what was going on, sped her chariot to where the hero and the giant fought.

"You cannot kill Alcyoneus while he stands on the ground that gave him birth," she cried.

On hearing these words, Heracles caught the giant in his arms. Hoisting him onto his back, Heracles strode away from the battle and on into a new territory, the giant all the while struggling futilely. There Heracles slew him with his great club.

Meanwhile, Athena had started in pursuit of a giant named Pallas. His brother Enceladus, who had a hundred arms, rushed to his aid. But though they fought side by side, their power was as nothing to the furious onslaught of the warrior goddess. She killed them both and triumphantly added the name of Pallas to her own, so that from then on men knew her as Pallas Athena. Enceladus she buried under the island of Sicily.

And so the victorious gods continued their rule on high Olympus.

A more peaceful contest settled a dispute between Athena and Poseidon, god of the sea. It concerned the city of Athens, named for the goddess. Poseidon demanded that its citizens take him for their special god. This angered Athena, and to avoid war between the powerful gods, the Athenians arranged for a contest between them, the citizens to decide which god had won.

Poseidon, as his part in the contest, struck a rock with

his trident, and a spring of salt water came gushing forth. The people were amazed and pleased by this miracle. But then Athena struck the butt of her spear against the ground, and a tree sprang up at once with spreading branches of gray-green leaves covered with small dark fruit. As the people marveled, the goddess showed them how to press the fruit to make oil. They found the oil good for flavoring their food, anointing their bodies, and burning in their lamps. Gratefully, they proclaimed Athena the winner of the contest, and ever after Athens was her city and the olive tree sacred to her.

The Story
of Aglauros

This story begins with the birth of a boy at Athens who,
like Athena, was born without a mother. He is supposed
to have been the son of Hephaestus, god of the forge. In
any case, Athena took pity on the motherless baby and
placed him in a chest woven of willow branches. She then
gave the chest into the care of three girls, daughters of
Cecrops, who was king of Athens, warning them not to
look inside it. Two of the girls, obedient to the gods,
heeded the warning. But in the heart of one, Aglauros,
raged a curiosity as great as Pandora's, who opened a cas-
ket and let loose all the plagues on the world.

At the first chance, Aglauros opened the chest, then
drew back in horror. A baby did lie asleep within it. But
coiled about the sleeping child was a deadly serpent. In
dread and fright, Aglauros slammed the lid down.

It wasn't long until Athena learned about Aglauros's defiance. The goddess's anger flamed up within her breast, and she hastened to find a way of punishing the girl for her curiosity.

One of Aglauros's sisters was named Herse. She was by far the prettiest of the three maidens, and one day, when she was leading a procession in honor of Athena, the god Hermes saw her and fell in love.

The god, descending through the clear air, wand in hand, followed the girls home. Aglauros saw him approaching, and she demanded to know who he was and what he wanted.

"I am Hermes, son of Zeus," he told her. "I am my father's messenger, and I long to speak with the fair Herse, for I love her well and would make her my wife. Tell me where I can find your sister so that I may go to her and declare my love."

Aglauros studied the god with the same covetous eyes that had pierced the secrets of the willow chest, and greed suddenly filled her heart. She demanded gold in exchange for telling where her sister was. Then she made Hermes depart from their dwelling, telling him not to return until he had the gold with him.

The Warrior Goddess, seeking revenge against Aglauros and keeping watch upon her, had seen and heard the exchange between her and Hermes. So great was Athena's wrath that the aegis shook upon her breast. This was the girl who had spied upon the baby born without a mother, and now she was plotting to please a god for gold. Athena could not endure it.

Striding angrily away, she sought the abode of Envy. It was a horrid place. Weeds and trash littered the dooryard. No wind blew there, but the place was cold with a gray mist constantly closing in upon it. The sun never shone there.

Athena approached the sagging door of the hut and struck it with the butt of her spear. It swung open to reveal a dark interior—surely no fireglow had ever brightened it—from which came the stink of gore. As the gray light from the dooryard crept across the threshold and into the center of the hut, Athena beheld the hag Envy eating the flesh of snakes. The goddess, disgusted by the sight, turned her gaze away as Envy rose from her low stool, spilling the half-eaten snakes upon the floor. She moved slowly toward the doorway, and the goddess, bright and beautiful in her shining armor, stepped back in abhorrence.

Well might the goddess avoid contact with such a loathsome creature. Envy's breast was filled with bitterness and her tongue coated with poison. She never laughed except at others' pain, and she never slept for watching that no one should ever know success. Where men succeeded, she failed. Athena hated her, as did all gods and mortals. But now she needed her.

Her orders were brief. "Go to Aglauros, Cecrops's daughter, and poison her heart. This is my command."

Then she pressed her spear into the filthy ground and, lifting herself on it, flew up to high Olympus.

Envy watched her out of sight, then took up her own staff, all twisted round with thorns, and started for Athens. As she went, the grasses dried, the flowers withered, and the trees looked as if they had suffered a long drought.

At last she came to the lovely city, and her heart filled with gall as she looked upon it. Here all was beauty. It shone with art and wealth, and there was nothing Envy could do to bring it down. She all but wept with disappointment and frustration.

Shuffling on, she came to the house of Cecrops and to Aglauros's chamber. There she laid her scrawny hand upon the sleeping girl's breast and filled it with envy of the sister so soon to wed a god. In her dream, Aglauros saw Hermes in all his beauty, and she hated Herse, loved by such a god. Then Envy went away, having carried out the order of Athena.

Aglauros woke and her dream was still vivid to her. All that day her envy grew, and that night she dreamed again of the marriage of Hermes and Herse. By the time the second night had ended and her eyes opened to another dawn, she felt she would rather die than to see her sister so happy.

She went to Herse's room and seated herself on the threshold. When the god arrived he offered the gold to Aglauros so that he might speak to Herse and declare his love.

But she refused the gold and said, "Here I shall remain until you are gone again."

"So it shall be," said Hermes and he struck his wand against the door.

It opened slowly, and Aglauros tried to rise from the threshold to prevent the god by force from entering. But what was this? She could not move. She could feel a coldness and a thickening all through her. It crept up her body and all around her heart. She tried to cry out, but her lips refused to open. She had become solid rock, a dark stone without features, blocking the doorway.

For a moment, Hermes stood looking at her. Then he turned away and, soaring aloft on his winged sandals, returned to his father on Mount Olympus. The god's love, at best a transitory thing, had been blighted by the evil spirit of Herse's envious sister.

Thus did Athena avenge herself against a mortal who dared defy a god.

The Story of Perseus

A RASH PROMISE

Of the many heroes dear to Athena, none was greater than Perseus, son of Zeus.

Acrisius, king of Argos, had received an oracle which said that his daughter Danae would have a son who would cause his grandfather's death. This so frightened Acrisius that he had a tower built of bronze. There he imprisoned Danae, who was very beautiful, so that no man might ever wed her. But Zeus had already seen the maiden and fallen in love with her. He managed to visit her in a shower of gold. Later, when news was brought to Acrisius that his daughter had given birth to a baby boy, the king was as furious as he was frightened. But he knew better than to kill his grandson, who was named Perseus. This the gods would never forgive. Instead he ordered a wooden chest to be built, and when it was ready, he placed poor Danae and her baby inside the chest and fastened its lid down tight with bands of bronze. He then set the chest adrift upon the wide sea.

The chest bobbed and rocked on the water while inside it Danae talked to her baby, trying to still the panic that threatened to overwhelm her reason.

"Dear one, what terrible fate awaits us? What evil have we done that we should be treated so cruelly? You are asleep and do not feel my tears upon your cheeks. Nor do you hear the waters lapping so close beside us. I know not whether it be day or night. This bronze-bound box must be our bed—or coffin."

So she grieved during the long hours. All day and all night the chest drifted on the sea. Then there was a gentle bump, and the chest was still. Danae's heart quickened as hope filled it. They must have reached land and might yet be saved.

That day a fisherman named Dictys had risen with the dawn to fish. But as he approached the shore he saw something out where the tide ran up the beach. He quickened his pace until he reached the water's edge and saw a huge wooden chest bound with bronze.

Dictys waded into the surf and waited for a large lifting wave, and when it broke he pushed with all his might and ran the sea-soaked chest safely up the beach. Quickly he took up a rock and smashed the clasp. Raising the lid, he beheld the lovely young mother and her child cowering within.

Danae took his hand and rose stiffly to her feet. "Surely the gods have sent you," she said. "But I know not what is to become of us. We are lost and alone."

"My home is humble and childless," said the fisherman. "If you will come there with me, I know my good wife will make you and the baby welcome for as long as you wish to stay."

And so it came about that the king's daughter and the son of Zeus joined their fortunes with those of a simple fisherman and his wife. The years sped by happily, and then misfortune struck again.

The ruler of this island was an evil man named Polydectes. It chanced one day as he walked in a procession that his eyes caught sight of Danae, and instantly he fell in love with her. At once he followed her to the fisherman's cottage. Perseus, now a growing boy, quickly resented the king's advances toward his mother. Nor did Danae receive him kindly.

Now Polydectes could easily have had Perseus put to death and simply have made off with Danae. But Polydectes knew that in such a case Danae would end her own life, and he wanted her. It was plain to him that in order to have her, he must first get rid of Perseus.

"So fine a lad should not waste his life as a fisherman," the wily Polydectes told Danae. "Let me take him back to my court where he can learn the arts of war."

Danae, thinking the king had decided to withdraw his interest from her, and seeing the eager light which had sprung into her son's eyes at the king's words, reluctantly gave her consent. Perseus returned with Polydectes to his palace.

Many months went by and never once did Polydectes try to speak with Danae. Perseus's fears were put to rest.

Then one day the king announced to all the court that he would soon celebrate his birthday feast. Of course no one could come to the feast without bringing a gift. And Perseus had nothing to give. There had never been anything in Dictys's little cottage that a king would value. When the great day came Perseus stood miserably by as one after another offered their gifts to Polydectes. At last everyone within the feasting hall had approached the king—everyone except Perseus. All eyes turned to him, curious as to what the fisherman's foster son would offer.

Suddenly Perseus leaped to his feet. "I will bring you a better gift than any you have thus far received," he cried. "I will bring you the head of Medusa, the Gorgon."

There was a gasp from all the king's guests at this rash promise. But the king smiled; this was exactly what he had wanted. No one could face Medusa and live.

She was a monster, one of three sisters known far and wide because of the deadly power they possessed. Their faces were so hideous to behold that whoever gazed upon them was turned to stone. The hair of Medusa's head was a mass of writhing serpents. Two sisters were immortal and hence could not be killed. But Medusa was vulnerable. Yet who could kill Medusa without the god's help? And now Perseus in his anger and humiliation had promised to accomplish this impossible task.

The boy left the hall and began wandering seaward, the reckless valor he had just shown gone out of him. He walked like one in a dream or like one returning weary from a long day's work. His head fell forward, and his dragging feet trailed the sand behind him as he approached the shore. How should he start upon his mission? How could he find Medusa? What part of the world harbored such a horror? And even if he knew how to find her, how could he arrive there? He had no ship nor would he ever have one.

At last he came to where the sand was wet and hard, and there he paused and looked along the line of beach. Suddenly he stiffened and his eyes sharpened. A brightness was speeding toward him, and gradually within that radiant nimbus he saw the figure of a woman. But this was no mortal woman. She wore a helmet and carried a shield on one arm. In her other hand was a spear.

"Athena!" exclaimed Perseus. "The goddess Athena!"

Lightly she paused beside him with a rattle of arms and said, "Son of Zeus, hearken now to my words."

Too amazed for speech, Perseus was barely able to focus his wits on what the goddess was saying.

"You have made a rash promise to Polydectes. Not even Heracles can strike off Medusa's head. But when was youth other than rash and reckless? Still Zeus has taken pity on your foolish pride and has sent me to you. Other aid is also on the way. Yet test will be made of your own courage in the final trial." As she spoke, her gray eyes softened and a grudging smile made gentle the stern line of her mouth. The youth looked so defenseless, so untried, that Athena's heart was moved. After all, he was her brother.

Meeting her gaze at last, Perseus felt his own heart strengthened. Whatever test might be required of him, the gods were on his side; nothing was impossible now.

"Only tell me what I must do," he said.

"First you must obtain three things: a cap of darkness, winged sandals, and a magic wallet which exactly holds whatever you wish to put into it. All these are in the possession of the Nymphs of the North."

"And where are they?" asked Perseus.

"Only the Gray Women can give you the answer to that," Athena told him. "You must find the Gray Women first. There are three of them, and they possess but one eye among them. It will be necessary for you to go to where they are, wait your opportunity, and snatch the eye when one sister passes it to another. Then refuse to return it until they have told you the way to the Nymphs of the North."

"And how shall I find the Gray Women?" asked Perseus.

No sooner had the words left his lips when he felt a sudden rush of air beside him and, turning, saw Hermes in all his beauty.

"Hermes!" Perseus barely breathed the name.

The god smiled. "Yes, it is I, Hermes, messenger of Zeus, and I have come at his bidding to guide you to the Gray Women. They dwell beyond the River of Ocean.

The Father of Gods has also commanded me to give you this."

He handed Perseus the weapon he held, curved in the shape of a scimitar. It was the blade which had struck off the head of Argus.

Still greatly wondering, Perseus took the blade and tested its balance in his hand. Then he looked up at the god. "May Zeus forgive me for doubting his wisdom, but what use is a blade if one cannot look upon the Gorgon without turning into stone? Surely I must look upon her if I am to direct the gleaming bronze truly."

And now Athena spoke. "Here," she said, "is my shield. Use it as a mirror to reflect the Gorgon's head. Thus you will see to strike without looking upon her."

Perseus took the shield and slipped it on his own left arm. With scimitar and shield, and Hermes to guide him, all seemed assured. But still, he remembered, he had to find the Nymphs of the North and that depended on how quickly he could act to seize the single eye of the Gray Women.

THE SEARCH FOR MEDUSA

Athena vanished and Hermes took Perseus by the wrist. At the same moment he touched him with his wand, and the next thing the youth knew they were rising above the beach and winging out over the water. Higher and higher the god flew, holding Perseus firmly. At first the lad was frightened to see the world so far below him, then the exhilaration of flight filled him. The rush of wind, the sense of lightness, the joy of such freedom brought a smile to Perseus's lips. With Hermes floating beside him, he ran along the sky exulting in this new and wonderful power. And so, at last they came to the country of the Gray Women.

They spiraled down from the bright sky into a gray and misty world. Streamers of fog rose as when a warm sun touches glacial ice. But with Hermes to guide him, Perseus found his way through the mist to where a gloomy cave faced the sea. Before it sat three strange creatures. They had the bodies of great birds, yet their heads were human, and beneath the mighty wings that lay along their bodies were hands and arms. These were the Gray Women. Perseus hid himself and watched them for a few moments. Then he saw one of them put out her hand and another lay a single eye on the extended palm. He waited, and when in turn she made as if to pass the eye to her sister, Perseus dashed from his hiding place and took the eye into his own hand.

"Sister, give me the eye," said the one who had expected to receive it.

"But I have given it into your hand," said the other. "I felt you take it."

"Then it is lost to us, for I have it not."

Now a cry went up from all three. "Our eye, our eye. Give it back, give it back."

Perseus stepped forward. "It is I, Perseus, who has your eye, and I will return it when you have told me the way to the Nymphs of the North."

For a while they argued among themselves, for this was a secret they held sacred. At last, however, as the moments passed and they felt more and more keenly their loss, they decided to tell Perseus what they knew. The Nymphs of the North, they told him, dwelled in the country of the Hyperboreans, which lay at the back of the north wind.

With Hermes still beside him, Perseus flew to that northern land and found it a place of great merriment and feasting. Here Hermes took leave of Perseus, and the youth stayed for some time resting in the lovely gardens of the nymphs. They were glad to have him and would have kept him forever, but he begged to be allowed to leave to fulfill his promise.

As Athena had predicted, they gave him the directions for finding Medusa and three indispensable gifts. These were a cap of darkness, which rendered its wearer invisible; winged sandals very like those that Hermes wore; and a leather wallet which would exactly fit whatever was put into it.

Taking leave of the kindly nymphs, Perseus rose with his own wings and flew away to find Medusa.

He recognized her island at once, for all about it were shapes frozen into stone. Rabbits in the act of bounding away, a stag with antlers lifted, birds, and even people whom Medusa or one of her sisters had turned to stone.

Gliding lightly down, Perseus approached the rock on

which the three monsters sat. But he was careful to view them only in the mirror of Athena's shield. To his joy he saw that they were all asleep. Only the serpents coiling about Medusa's head slid and slithered as she slept. Cautiously, Perseus, wearing the cap of darkness, approached the sleeping monster.

Suddenly Athena was again beside him. She guided his hand as he raised the scimitar. The deadly bronze struck down, smiting the hideous head from its body. The hiss of the blade woke the other two. As the other Gorgons sprang up, Perseus thrust Medusa's head into his wallet. Swiftly the winged sandals carried him beyond the sisters' furious reach, and in seconds he was over the ocean alone.

THE GARDENS OF THE HESPERIDES

Seeking his way homeward, Perseus flew across the world until he came to its western reaches, even to the spot where the tired horses of the sun descend with the fiery chariot into the sea.

This was the land which Atlas ruled, a giant who bore the sky upon his shoulders. Besides his many cattle herds, Atlas owned a most wonderful garden in the center of which was a tree bearing golden apples. The tree was tended by a group of lovely maidens known as the Hesperides.

Perseus floated down into the garden and approached Atlas, bowed under the weight of the sky. He took the cap of darkness from his head and addressed the giant.

"You see before you Perseus, son of Zeus. I have come here from the other side of the world, and I ask that you let me rest within this garden."

Atlas did not answer at once. A long time ago he had received an oracle that said his wondrous apple tree would one day lose all its gold and that the thief would be a son of Zeus. To protect his golden apples, therefore, he had built a wall around his garden and placed a dragon to keep watch under the tree. Now, here was a son of Zeus—surely come to rob him.

Sudden fury filled the giant. He shifted the sky so that he could raise his bowed head. The clouds trembled, while the stars behind the blue curtain of daylight were thrown off their course, and confusion reigned in heaven.

"Liar," cried Atlas, "begone from here. I care not whose son you are or where you come from." With that, he bent his knee and gave the hero a rude shove. Perseus tried to stand his ground, but who can stand against the strength of Atlas?

Then Perseus said, "Your hospitality shall be rewarded. I have something here which I wish to show you."

He turned his head and, opening the leather wallet, lifted from it the hideous head of Medusa. Atlas, whose curiosity had been aroused at Perseus's words, was watching eagerly to see what he might have in that sack. Too late, he recognized it for what it was. Immediately his feet

began to spread like molten lava oozing from a deep crack in the earth. Joining together, they hardened into solid stone and a line of hills. His arms, reaching up and out to steady the sky, became mountain ranges running off to right and left above the hills. The hair of his head became a forest growing from the range's summit. And where Atlas had stood a mountain rose with the sky upon it.

That night Perseus rested in the garden of the Hesperides. When the dawn opened its rosy chamber and the horses of the sun began to mount the sky, the hero woke and fastened on his winged sandals. Then he armed himself with Athena's shield and Hermes's sword and, again protected by the cap of darkness, flew away from the garden and across the seas in search of his homeland. At last he came to a vast mainland which stretched in all directions as far as he could see. This was the land of Ethiopia in Africa.

ANDROMEDA

Gliding down the sky, Perseus beheld a statue of a maiden close against a stony cliff. It was of such great beauty that he hastened to inspect it at close hand. What was his wonder as he drew near to find that its dark loveliness was not stone, as he had supposed, but living flesh. The maiden was bound to the rock by heavy chains, and great was her distress. Tears shone on her cheeks, which were as soft and smooth as brown velvet. Perseus flew around her several times, making sure no monster might be lurking near. At last, seeing only the rocky shore and the suffering maiden, he dropped to earth and, removing the cap of darkness from his head, approached her.

"Dear girl, what evil have you done that you should suffer a fate like that of Prometheus? Do you, too, await the eagle of Zeus, or may some hero free you from your torment? If the latter, then may it be I, Perseus, son of Zeus, for your beauty has captured my heart, and I would gladly risk my life to free you."

She turned her head to look upon him, then lowered her eyes shyly. When she spoke it was in a gentle voice shaking with fright.

"I am Andromeda, daughter of King Cepheus, ruler of Ethiopia. My mother Cassiopea in a moment of vanity boasted that her beauty was greater than that of the sea nymphs. In anger, they afflicted the country with a scourge. Rain ceased to fall and the crops died. At last the people could endure their sufferings no longer and demanded that my father do something to relieve them. He sought counsel of the sea nymphs, and they, pitiless, said they would lift the scourge only if I were given over to the Monster of the Sea. It will come shortly to claim me as its bride or to devour me. Between those fates there is no choice." Her words ceased as sobs shook her frail body and the cruel chains binding it.

"Dear Andromeda," said Perseus, "surely a better fate awaits you. With the help of the gods I have slain the

Gorgon Medusa, and with their help I shall slay the
Monster of the Sea. Then will I claim you as my bride if
you will have me."

Andromeda looked at him, and now there was hope in
her eyes. "Brave Perseus, only save me and I will love you
faithfully to the end of my days."

His heart strengthened by her words, Perseus donned
again the cap of darkness and took his stand upon a shiny
rock the sea waves washed with white spray. Athena's
shield lay on the sand at the feet of Andromeda, but the
scimitar of Hermes was in Perseus's right hand, and the
blood-soaked wallet containing the head of Medusa hung
from his shoulder.

Perseus's eyes searched the turbulent waters, and after
a few moments he saw a change on their surface. Something was cleaving them and flinging up a fine mist as it
came. He caught the glint of shiny scales and then a tail,
pointed like a spearhead, rose out of the water. The
Monster of the Sea was coming to claim its prey.

Perseus flung himself into the air and flew out to where
the monster's long body wallowed in the heaving waters.
Hovering above it, he saw a space between the shoulder
scales. Darting down, he drove the scimitar in at that un-
defended spot. The beaten water hissed furiously as it
met the flame streaming from the monster's mouth. The
awful creature circled swiftly and half rose from the sea
as it tried to clutch its tormenter in its clawed front feet.
But Perseus, still invisible, was out of reach. Then seeing
another chance, he flew in under the monster's great jaw

and lunged a stroke into its thin underbelly. The blue waters reddened as the dark blood poured out. Again and again Perseus thrust the blade between the monster's scaly plates, but still it came on strongly, swimming in its own blood as it made for the shore. With a mighty effort it flung itself out of the water and began crawling up the sand. Andromeda cried out most piteously, for it was making straight toward her.

Perseus dropped the scimitar and opened the wallet.

"Andromeda!" he cried. "Close your eyes and do not open them until I give you leave."

Dutifully the princess closed her eyes, and Perseus lifted the Gorgon's head from the wallet, all the while keeping his eyes safely turned away. At the same instant he swept off the cap of darkness and gave a loud cry to draw the monster's attention. It swept its gaze to where the cry had sounded, and instantly, where there had been a frightful creature dragging its bleeding length across the sand, there was now only a long, flat stone.

As Perseus slipped the head back into the wallet, he became aware of shouting behind him. His whole thought had been for Andromeda, and he had not noticed that King Cepheus, Queen Cassiopea, and hundreds of their subjects had gathered at a safe distance to watch the conflict between the hero and the monster. They came running up the strand. King Cepheus and Queen Cassiopea stretched out their arms to clasp the daughter who had been so miraculously rescued and restored to them. They heaped praise and thankfulness upon the hero as they undid Andromeda's fetters. When the last chain fell, Andromeda swayed forward and Perseus took her in his arms.

"Name your reward," said King Cepheus. "Though it be my kingdom, it shall be yours."

"I want no reward but what I hold here," said Perseus, tightening his arms around Andromeda.

"She is yours," declared the king. "Your marriage feast shall be celebrated this very day."

Before going to the palace of King Cepheus, Perseus raised two altars on the sandy beach. One was to Athena and the other to Hermes. Then all that crowd of people did honor to the altars. Even the sea nymphs, won over by Perseus's heroism, laid upon them pieces of bright coral, the brittle flowers of ocean. Forever after this was a sacred spot for the Ethiopians.

There was one among the court who had not witnessed the fight between Perseus and the monster. Phineus, the betrothed of Andromeda, had lacked the courage to defend her and had remained safely at the palace. While his grief at the loss of his lovely bride was great, it was not enough to overcome his cowardice. Assuming Andromeda had met her fate, he was startled to hear shouts of joy from the crowd returning to the palace. And when Phineus learned that his promised bride was alive and safe, but a promised bride no longer, his fury was as great as his cowardice had been.

Preparations for the marriage feast went swiftly forward. Andromeda's maidens ranged the meadows gathering flowers to decorate the hall. The finest animals in the king's herds were slaughtered and set above the roasting coals. Musicians were summoned, and also storytellers who would take part in all the festivities and weave them into stories for the delight of generations to come.

When all was ready the feasting began. Perseus with Andromeda beside him sat at the head of the board with King Cepheus and Queen Cassiopea. When the merriment had reached its height, Phineus rose at his place and hailed Perseus in a voice heavy with scorn, a coward's scorn before courage.

"Bride stealer!" he cried, waving his bronze-tipped lance above his head. "Who could not succeed when the gods support him? Andromeda was mine before they meddled in this affair, and mine she will continue to be."

Suddenly the feast was in an uproar.

"Silence," the king roared, and at his command, the hall was suddenly still except for a low murmuring like the growling of sullen dogs deprived of their prey. "What madness is this, Phineus? My daughter has been spared to me, but not through any act of yours. Where were you when the Monster of the Sea came up on the land? Cowering here and grieving futilely. Had you prepared to defend Andromeda and bravely stood between her and the monster, even if then Perseus had come in time to save you both, even then I would grant your case as her betrothed. But you made no move to save her, and so I say you have no claim upon her now. She is rightfully the bride of Perseus, and so it shall be."

The king sat down, and for a moment Phineus stood at his place, hesitating. Then, making up his mind, he aimed his lance and hurled it straight at Perseus. But the hero, who had never taken his eyes from his rival, saw the throw and flung himself aside. The spearhead pierced the chair on which he had been sitting.

Perseus, all warrior, quickly wrenched the spear from the wood and hurled it back. Phineus, too, dodged it, and it whistled past him to pierce the skull of one of his supporters. Now every man was on his feet, and every one was against Perseus, the pale stranger. Only three within that hall were on his side: his bride, her father, and her mother.

Perseus put his back against a marble column and bravely fought. Athena's shield caught many a lance, and the scimitar of Hermes cut down those men who rashly came within its reach. But there were too many; Perseus could feel his sword arm weakening as his muscles tired. He thought of Medusa's head and how easily he could win this battle if only he could draw it forth and hold it high. But there, huddled at the head of the table were Andromeda and her parents, watching the unequal battle with fearful eyes. They, too, would be turned to stone, for in the deafening noise of the conflict there was no way he could warn them.

Suddenly a brightness shone within the hall and Athena stood among them. Perseus saw her, but his enemies had their backs to her and so were unaware of the goddess. Fending off blows, Perseus saw Athena lead the king out of the hall, Andromeda and the queen following. They were safe, and now Perseus, putting the marble column between him and his attackers, opened the wallet and lifted forth the terrible head.

In an instant, the hall was filled with an awesome silence. Of all that shrieking horde, only Phineus remained flesh and bone. Perhaps the shining Athena had alerted his glance, for now he was looking to where the royal family had been seated, noting their absence, and wondering if some trick had been played on him.

It was then Perseus let out a cry. "Great coward, look this way."

Phineus swung about and his eyes sought the thing that Perseus held above his head. And now within the hall only Perseus breathed. Holding his gaze averted, he slipped the Gorgon's head inside the wallet, and wearily left.

So Perseus won his bride and with her returned to his island home where the evil Polydectes ruled.

Proudly, his bride beside him, he approached the little cottage where he and the lovely Danae had been so kindly received. The aged Dictys was sitting on a bench beside the door. The old man looked sadly forlorn as Perseus led Andromeda up to him. But at the sight of Perseus he rose stiffly, fear suddenly taking the place of sorrow on his lined face.

Perseus, understanding, laughed happily. "This is no ghost you see here, Dictys. It is I, Perseus, returned from the back of the north wind. And here," drawing her gently forward, "is my wife, the Princess Andromeda."

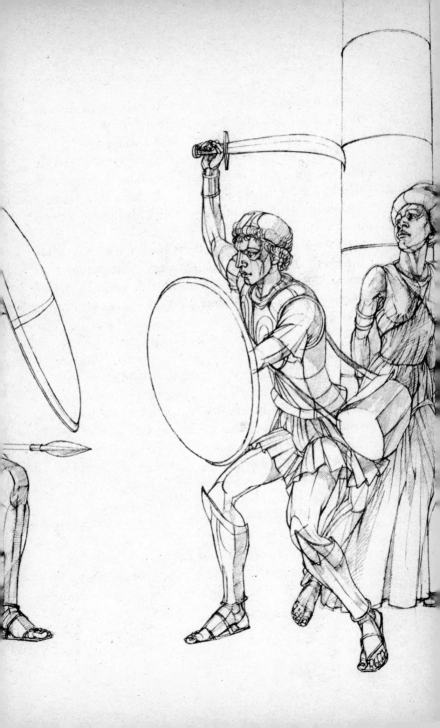

Dictys hardly glanced at the lovely girl smiling shyly at him. Instead, he threw himself upon Perseus's shoulder while terrible weeping racked his old body.

"Ah, Perseus, woe is upon us," he lamented. "Hardly had you gone away when Polydectes came here and carried Danae off to his palace. Now she remains a prisoner within the women's quarters until such time as he sees fit to make her his wife by force."

At these words, Perseus's heart swelled with wrath. He shifted the bloody wallet hanging from one shoulder. At the same time he placed Andromeda's hand in that of Dictys's wife, who had come from the cottage on hearing their voices.

"Take care of her even as you did my mother until such time as I come back to you," said Perseus.

Then he whirled and started toward the palace.

Perseus could hardly have planned it better. He found the king and all his court within the feasting hall. For a moment he watched them, studying the scene of revelry. Then Polydectes noticed him. The king gave a start, and a look came into his eyes not unlike that which had rested in the gaze of Dictys a short while before. And Perseus responded to that look in much the same way.

"Hail, Polydectes," he cried, but now there was no laughter in his voice. "This is no ghost you see before you, but Perseus, son of Zeus and Danae, returned after making good his promise to you." He held the wallet high. "Here is the head of Medusa. Free Danae and swear never again to molest her and it will be yours, if so you wish."

"Liar," yelled Polydectes back at him, "there never was a Medusa. Such tales are for children or for fools. As to the fair Danae, she shall be my wife before this day's sun has set."

A clamor rose within the hall as the men of the court, all loyal to Polydectes, started toward Perseus. Wasting no time, the hero opened the wallet and held up the head of the Gorgon, being careful to keep his own eyes averted.

"We will see who is the fool now, Polydectes," he cried.

No words answered him for all within the hall had been changed to stone.

Then Perseus found his mother in her chamber and led her joyfully away and back to the little cottage where Andromeda and the old couple awaited them.

Later that day Perseus, carrying the shield and the scimitar, with the wallet flung over his shoulder, walked to the beach where he had stood despairing on the day he had made his promise to Polydectes. Now he came to the same spot, this time with a heart full of triumph and thanksgiving.

He had not long to wait. Suddenly, as before, there was a shining and Athena stood before him. Her gray eyes smiled into those of Perseus as she slipped the shield from his arm and took it on her own.

"Brave Perseus," she said in ringing tones, "you have deserved the favor of the gods. Men will sing of your great deeds throughout all the generations to come."

"Goddess," replied Perseus, "it is not within mortal power to repay your kindness. Yet will I try if only you will command me."

In answer Athena said, "Turn away your head and hand me the wallet."

Perseus obeyed and in an instant heard the goddess say, "Behold!"

He turned his glance back again and gasped at what he saw. The head of the Gorgon, Medusa, was now implanted in the very center of Athena's shield. And there it was to remain forevermore, its evil power ended.

Shortly thereafter Hermes appeared to reclaim the scimitar. The cap of darkness and the winged sandals he took, too, and in time returned them to the Hyperboreans at the back of the north wind.

FULFILLMENT OF THE ORACLE

During all the years in which Perseus had grown to manhood, old Acrisius, his grandfather, had lived contentedly. He was certain that Perseus must be safely dead and the oracle no longer a threat.

But now Perseus decided that he wanted to return to the land of his birth and to take his bride there. Danae wanted to return with them and be reconciled with her father. Before leaving the island, Perseus placed the good Dictys on the throne of Polydectes, sure that his rule would be both kind and just, for that was the nature of the old man.

The three arrived in Argos only to find that Acrisius had left the city, and no one knew where he had gone or when he would be back.

While Perseus was awaiting the old king's return, he learned of an athletic contest being held by the king of Larissa in the north. It was a contest of such importance that Perseus wanted to take part in it. Leaving Andromeda in the care of Danae, he started out. He traveled for many days and at last came to the site of the contest. It was a large field with seats arranged at one side for the king and his guests. Perseus entered himself for the discusthrowing, a feat in which he excelled. But he did not give his name, nor did he go to greet the king who sat surrounded by his guests. That would come later—if he won. Thus Perseus had no chance to learn that one of those guests was his grandfather Acrisius. Nor did the old king recognize in the fine athlete about to take the field the newborn baby he had treated so cruelly.

When it came Perseus's turn at the discus-throwing, he stepped confidently forward, the heavy round plate balanced expertly on his right hand. Silence settled over the field as he drew his hand back, then flung the discus forward with tremendous force. Straight down the field it went. Then suddenly, as if an unseen hand had nudged it, the discus veered off at an angle, striking one of the king's guests, who fell from his seat, his skull crushed. Dazed, unbelieving, Perseus ran forward.

"Whom have I struck?" he cried. "You saw?" he said to the king, forgetting in his anguish how a king should be approached. "What caused the discus to veer as it did?"

The king spoke kindly to the young man whose grief was so evident. "It was the will of the gods," he said. "The man you have just killed is Acrisius, king of Argos. The oracle is fulfilled, Perseus."

The hero stayed in Larissa long enough to see his grandfather buried with the dignity befitting a king, even a bad one, and then he returned to Argos with his sad news.

Danae felt sorrow for the loss of her father and grieved that he had died at Perseus's hand. Yet the painful memory of those long and terrifying hours in the wooden chest somewhat tempered her grief.

As for Perseus, he and Andromeda lived happily all the rest of their lives. His son, Perses, became ruler of the Persians, who took their name from his.

BELLEROPHON AND PEGASUS

One would expect a warrior goddess to be deeply concerned with all the arts and implements of war. To what extent is shown by the help Athena gave Bellerophon when he stood in great need of it.

Now in those old times, a man's most important possession after his weapons was his horse. Only the greatest heroes had horses though; common soldiers fought battles on foot. It was Poseidon, god of the sea, who gave horses to men, and these first horses must have been white, for even now on a windy day we can see white manes tossing above blue ocean waters. But it was Athena who invented the art of training horses for use by man. Indeed, it was she who invented the chariots in which heroes rode to battle.

Bellerophon was the son of Glaucus, king of Corinth, a city not far from Argos where Perseus was born. In many ways Bellerophon's story is similar to that of Perseus, who unwittingly played an important part in Bellerophon's fate.

When Perseus struck off the terrible head of Medusa, he was so engrossed in getting the head stuffed safely into the magic wallet that he failed to notice a miracle taking place where Medusa's body lay in a pool of blood.

Out of the corpse of that terrible creature there rose a beautiful white horse with huge wings sweeping back from his withers. This was Pegasus, created out of the blood and body of a monster, a winged horse forever after to be the symbol of poetic imagination. For this noble animal flew straight to Mount Helicon and there, to entertain the Muses who dwelled on it, Pegasus struck the ground with his front hoof. Immediately a spring gushed forth. This spring, Hippocrene, was to become the source of poetic inspiration. To this day we sometimes say of a fine poet, "He must have been borne aloft on the wings of Pegasus."

The fame of the winged horse quickly spread throughout all the lands of Greece, and it was every boy's dream to possess him someday. But Pegasus would let no one come near him. At the first sight of an approaching human being, he would spread his great wings and, pawing the air with his front hooves, rise into the heavens, his mane and tail streaming like cloud mist along the mountaintops.

Among the boys who most longed for Pegasus was King Glaucus's son, Bellerophon. At last one day when he had come to full manhood, he sought out the seer Polyidus and asked what he should do to conquer the winged horse.

"Go this night to the temple of Athena and there sleep near her altar."

Bellerophon took the seer's advice. As soon as it was dark, he slipped away to the dark grove where the tall columns of the temple loomed. As he stretched himself for sleep there, he wondered if the goddess might resent his taking such liberties with her sacred ground. However, it was scarcely possible that Polyidus, a seer who always spoke with the voice of a god, would advise a mortal to do wrong. So, clearing his mind of all anxiety, Bellerophon fell asleep and began to dream.

The goddess Athena stood beside him. In her hand was a golden bridle.

"Go at once to the spring Pirene. There you will find Pegasus. Slip this bridle over his head, and he will be yours to command."

The dream ended and Bellerophon awoke. The temple

was totally dark; he was alone. But when he put out his hand, he touched something. Eagerly he took it up. It was a bridle!

Bellerophon hastened outside where the bright moon was making shadows in the grove. The bridle glistened in the moonlight.

Pirene lay at the edge of Corinth, and Bellerophon lost no time in going there. As he approached the spot, he stopped suddenly, and his breath stopped with him. Before him in the shining moonlight stood a dazzling white horse. His lovely head lowered to the fountain's brink, he was drinking from the spring, his great wings folded along his back. Bellerophon, bridle in hand, took a cautious step toward the wondrous steed. Instantly Pegasus flung up his head, and silvery water streamed from his soft muzzle. Trembling, he watched the young hero's approach, his dark eyes wide. He seemed about to wheel and fly away.

Moving quietly and steadily, Bellerophon came up to Pegasus and laid a hand upon his shining neck. The horse whinnied softly and dropped his nose to the youth's shoulder. Bellerophon quickly slipped the golden bridle onto his head. Pegasus was his!

Some time after this, quite by chance and without ever intending it, Bellerophon caused the death of his brother. Though innocent of any crime, Bellerophon had enemies at court who were jealous of his good looks and athletic prowess, to say nothing of his possession of the winged horse. They worked against Bellerophon so viciously that King Glaucus was forced to exile his son from Corinth.

The youth found refuge in Tiryns. Here the king, Proetus, ritually cleansed Bellerophon from any least taint of crime and quickly came to love him. So, unfortunately, did Proetus's queen, Anteia. She took note of the athlete's body, of his regular features and wide brow. She especially admired his golden hair, which curled close to his head like the tightly coiled flowers of the hyacinth. For a while she managed to control her passion, but at last it overcame her. Sure of her own beauty, and never dreaming that Bellerophon did not feel the same passion for her, she spoke boldly of her love.

"Ever since you first came here to Tiryns and my eyes beheld you, I have thought of no one else but you, Bellerophon. I have no wish to live longer without you. Therefore let us flee to some country where we can enjoy our love to the end of our lives without fear."

Bellerophon was shocked at this revelation. He hardly knew how to reply to the queen. To deny her would be to insult her, but to encourage her would be even more dangerous. Besides, he had no wish to encourage her.

"Noble lady," he said at last, "your words are the richest flattery of my life and I am humbled by your declaration of love. Yet I beg you never mention it again. Your husband, King Proetus, is my friend. He is also my host. What you propose is unthinkable."

At these words, Anteia's face reddened with humilia-

.tion. Her eyes, so lately soft with love, narrowed, and she
bestowed upon the youth a look so filled with hatred that
it chilled him. Then she whirled about and sped from his
presence.

That evening when Anteia and the king had retired to
their apartment in the palace, she said, "There is something I have been wanting to tell you, Proetus, but until
now shame has sealed my lips."

"What could possibly cause my queen to feel shame?"
demanded her husband.

She swung about from the little table where she had
been carefully arranging her jewels.

"Your guest Bellerophon," she replied. "He has declared his love for me and has urged me to flee with him."

For a moment the king stood shocked and unbelieving.
As the queen continued to study him with level, un-
abashed eyes, rage swept across his face and the veins stood
out on his temples.

"I thought you should know," she murmured, turning
back to her jewel box.

All that night the king tossed and turned and could not
sleep. His rage at his guest's betrayal consumed him. He
longed to go at once and thrust his sword through Bellerophon, because, of course, he believed what his wife
had told him.

One thing alone prevented his making an end of the
youth that very night—Bellerophon was his guest, and a
host might not do violence to a guest beneath his roof
without incurring the wrath of the gods. So Proetus bided

his time and tried to think of some other way to work his vengeance on the hero.

One day Proetus approached his guest, a sealed letter in his hand.

"Bellerophon, you have often expressed a wish to repay me in some way for the hospitality I have shown you. The pleasure of your company has always been reward enough for me," went on the treacherous king. "But there is a favor you can perform which I should much appreciate."

"Name it, Proetus, and I will fulfill your mission, or die in the attempt."

"Well spoken," replied the king. He held out the letter. "Here is a message for my father-in-law, King Iobates of Lycia. Will you deliver it for me? The way to him is beset with heavy dangers else I would send an ordinary messenger. But with the winged horse, you can go there easily. And may the gods give you good speed."

Bellerophon took the letter and went to bridle Pegasus, all unsuspecting that the wily Proetus had written Iobates that the bearer of the letter had tried to seduce Anteia, and he should be put to death.

Iobates greeted Bellerophon warmly, and for nine days, as hospitality demanded, he treated the youth most cordially, not asking who he was or why he had come. It was not until the tenth day that he put the question.

"Who are you whom the gods have favored with the winged horse? Word has reached me that a son of Glaucus in Corinth has tamed Pergasus. Are you then he?"

"Yes, oh king, I am Bellerophon."

"Your presence honors my kingdom," replied Iobates. "But why have you chosen to come here?"

Bellerophon drew the letter from his robe and handed it to the king. "Here is a message from Proetus, your son-in-law."

Iobates took the letter and withdrew to his private quarters to read what his son-in-law had written. He was glad he had done so, for the contents of the letter were so shocking that he could not have concealed their effect from his guest. He, too, had come to admire this young man in the time he had been in Lycia. It seemed incredible to Iobates that Anteia, his daughter, should have suffered insult from one who seemed so manly and noble. Yet here it was plainly stated by none other than that daughter's husband. Certainly Bellerophon must die. But how?

A dilemma faced Iobates much like the one that Proetus had evaded. How could he put to death a guest within his house? The gods would surely punish such behavior. The only way out for Iobates was to send the young man on a deadly mission and thus avoid direct responsibility for his death. That very day he summoned the hero to him.

"Bellerophon, I have a service to ask of you, one which will test your courage and win you undying fame if you succeed in it."

"What would you have me do?"

"A fearful monster is ravaging my kingdom, and I have

no one to send against it whom the gods favor as they favor you. This monster, who is known as the Chimaera, is part goat, part lion, and part snake. It breathes fire so that no man can get close enough to kill it."

"I will gladly take on this task," declared Bellerophon. "And if the gods are still with me, I will slay your Chimaera."

He bridled Pegasus, mounted him, and flew off into the heart of Lycia. It did not take him long to locate the fire-breathing monster. It was lying near its lair at the base of a mountain. Around it lay the bones of its victims.

Pegasus flew toward it swiftly while Bellerophon fitted an arrow to his bow. The monster, seeing the great white horse spiraling down from the blue sky, lashed the ground with its huge snake's tail and, lifting its lion's head, sent forth a column of fire. But the flames could not reach the winged horse circling above it. Bellerophon shot arrow after arrow into the hideous body, and at last the monster lay dead.

Iobates was overjoyed to have the Chimaera destroyed, and he ordered a feast to celebrate the victory. But he was still determined to rid the world of this stranger who had dared to offer insult to his daughter. Next day he had another mission for the hero.

"Bellerophon," he began, "a tribe neighbor to my kingdom, the Solymi, have been raiding my borders and causing much suffering to my people. I have sent my army against them, and though the Solymi are vanquished for

a while, they come swarming back again. Do you think
you might end this tribe's threat to my kingdom?"

Bellerophon eagerly reassured the king, and, mounted
on Pegasus, he sought out and routed the fierce Solymi.
It was the same when Iobates sent him against the Amazons, a tribe of warlike women. He returned triumphant
from that campaign also.

Now Iobates was desperate. It seemed that no hazard
was great enough to put an end to Bellerophon. Therefore he must undertake the deed himself. To that end, he
sent his army to ambush the youth one day when he was
hunting, riding Pegasus along the ground as on an ordinary horse.

Approaching a narrow pass, Bellerophon was suddenly
attacked by armed men. They would have dragged him
from his horse and killed him, but Pegasus, flailing with
his front hooves, spread his great wings and rose swiftly
out of reach. Then back and forth over the armed forces
of Iobates he flew while Bellerophon slaughtered the soldiers. At last they flung down their arms and fled, and
Bellerophon returned to the palace to tell the king how
his own soldiers had laid an ambush for him.

It was all a mistake, Iobates declared, and promised to
punish the officer in command of the soldiers. To prove
his innocence, he offered Bellerophon his other daughter,
Philonoe, in marriage with half his kingdom as her dowry.
Iobates had wisely decided by now that Bellerophon was,
indeed, a darling of the gods and that it would be dangerous to do him injury.

So Bellerophon remained in Lycia, happy with his bride, and his father-in-law never again plotted him any woe.

He could have been happy all the rest of his life if arrogance had not consumed him. Thinking over his exploits, Bellerophon quite forgot to whom he owed his many triumphs. He forgot that it was Athena who had made his fame possible by giving him the winged horse. He began to boast of his victories and at last began to think himself as great as the very gods. Why, then, should he remain in Lycia? Why should he not mount Pegasus and fly to high Olympus, there to share the company of the Immortals?

One day, with this purpose in mind, he mounted his winged steed and began spiraling up and up until the heights of Olympus were within his view. But the gods were witnessing his approach. Furious that any mortal should be so presumptuous, Zeus sent a gadfly to sting Pegasus. The winged horse lurched backward when he felt the sudden sting. Bellerophon, unprepared for such a maneuver, was flung from his back and fell to Earth. He was lamed by the fall, and for the rest of his life he wandered homeless and friendless, for no one would befriend anyone whom the gods had scorned.

As for Pegasus, some say he returned to Corinth and the spring of Pirene. Other legends declare that Zeus gave him to Eos, goddess of the dawn. One thing is certain, for us today he dwells among the stars as a constellation.

The Search for the Golden Fleece

THE MAN WITH ONE SANDAL

The man with one sandal! He it was whom King Pelias feared. The king had received an oracle warning him that a man with one sandal would take over his kingdom and ultimately cause his death.

King Pelias had every reason for dread. He had himself stolen the kingdom from his brother Aeson, who had inherited the throne when their father died. A thief's conscience is always a guilty one, so Pelias wore his crown with fear and foreboding.

The defrauded brother had a son named Jason. When Jason had grown to man's estate he decided to visit Iolcus, where his uncle reigned, and demand the return of the kingdom. To this end he started out one winter day from his aging father's home, walking down the coast of Thessaly toward the harbor city where Pelias was king.

He might have waited for a better season. Snow lay upon the mountaintops and every stream was swollen from the winter rains. But youth is impatient, and destiny does not wait upon a season. For Jason the time had come to demand his own.

He was near the city of Iolcus when the widest and swiftest stream of all rushed between him and his goal. Seeking a ford, Jason followed the riverbank to the very slopes of Mount Pelion. Near the entrance to a heavily wooded ravine, he decided it would be safe to attempt a crossing. The water was swift and icy and the boulders under his feet treacherously insecure. In midstream one of them turned as Jason set his foot on it, and in the struggle to maintain his balance in the swiftly flowing river one of his sandals was wrenched off. He thought little of the incident since he was so near the end of his journey, but stumbled on across the stream. In a little while he entered the city of Iolcus:

Ever since he had received that oracle, Pelias had posted a man at the entrance to the city whose duty it was to inspect everyone to make sure that both his feet were shod. If ever a man should arrive with one foot bare, it was to be reported at once to the king.

Of course Jason knew nothing of this. So he never noticed that as he passed through the city gate a man gave him a startled look and then sped off. Seeking the palace, Jason walked along slowly, eyeing with interest all the many wonders of the largest city he had ever seen. By the time he reached the marketplace, a crowd had gathered there, the king at its center.

Though Jason had never laid eyes on his uncle, he had no difficulty in recognizing Pelias. His robes, his bearing, and the guards who stood near him, all indicated that this was Pelias, unrightful king of Iolcus.

Jason strode boldly forward until he stood so close to his uncle that the guards' attention tautened, and they moved to intercept him. But Pelias held up a hand, and the soldiers returned to their former positions.

Jason was the first to speak. "I bring you greetings from your brother Aeson," he said.

Pelias inclined his head graciously. "My brother is fortunate in having such a manly messenger. Are you the captain of a king's guard? You look the very stuff of heroes. Tell me, who is your sire that I may envy him?"

A proud look crossed Jason's face. "My sire, oh king, is none other than your brother Aeson. I am his son, Jason."

For just an instant fear stood in the king's eyes. Then he smiled and put forth his hand to Jason. "You are welcome, Jason."

But Jason did not take his uncle's hand. "Before you welcome me, you had better hear the reason for my coming. I wish you to surrender to me the governing of this kingdom which by right belongs to my father. He is too aged now to assume it, and so he has delegated me his heir. You, Pelias, may keep for yourself all the riches the crown has brought to you—all the flocks and all the gold. I ask only that you surrender your kingship to me."

A wily look settled upon the king's face. "It seems a reasonable offer," he answered. "I keep my riches and give up my power. But it is a bargain which needs getting used to. Let us retire to the palace where we can discuss this matter in greater detail and privacy. You are indeed welcome there, Jason."

Again the king extended his hand, and this time Jason took it. Followed by the guard and members of the court, Jason and his uncle strolled as comrades toward the palace of Iolcus.

After he had bathed, annointed his body with scented oils, and donned the clothing which Pelias had ordered placed for him—raiment suitable to the nephew of a king —Jason went at once to his uncle's private apartment, where he was greeted most cordially.

"Jason," began Pelias, "I am inclined to make that bargain with you, for I too am aging. And though I have a son to follow me, I can easily see that you would never allow Acastus to rule where you considered yourself the rightful heir."

"You judge me rightly, Pelias," said Jason grimly.

The king sighed like one helpless to change his fortunes, and a wistful smile hid the black intent of his heart.

"I will peaceably surrender the kingdom to you, Jason, on one condition. You must bring me the Golden Fleece. Lately a ghost has bothered my sleep, demanding that the Fleece be brought here from Colchis, where King Aeetes guards it jealously. Bring me the Golden Fleece and you shall be king of Iolcus."

Jason leaped to his feet, his eyes shining. Here was a challenge to fire the heart of any young hero. To return the Fleece from far-flung Asia to the land from which it came! What glory would attend such an undertaking! In his contemplation of this magnificent adventure, young Jason quite forgot, or chose to overlook, the hazards attendant upon such an undertaking. He entirely failed to question the motive behind Pelias's desire to have the Fleece. He never saw in that desire a wish to rid himself of the one threat to his throne.

THE GOLDEN RAM

The fleece which Jason was now determined to go in search of had had a long and tragic history. This began when Phrixus, son of King Athamas, was a little boy. Athamas, having grown tired of his first wife, sent her away when he fell in love with Ino, a daughter of Cadmus. When a son was born to Ino, she began to look upon Phrixus with hatred, for he as the elder son would inherit the kingdom when Athamas died, and Ino intended the inheritance for her own child. So she began to plot the death of Phrixus.

It happened that that very year the harvest failed. The grain dried up before it could ripen, and the fruit withered on the vine. Ino saw her advantage in this situation.

She went to consult a soothsayer and returned to tell the king that only the sacrifice of his son Phrixus would appease the gods so that they would allow the earth to become fruitful again.

Athamas was shocked by the oracle and refused to listen to the urgings of Ino. But at last the people's sufferings became so great that they flocked to the palace and demanded that the boy be sacrificed so that their own children should not starve. Of course Ino had made certain that the oracle should be known throughout the kingdom. Fearful for his very throne, Athamas yielded to their demands, and Phrixus, along with his sister Helle, was led to the temple where the sacrifice was to take place. But just as the priest raised the knife that would end the boy's life, a wondrous golden ram appeared beside the altar. He ordered both children to climb upon his back and take hold of his fleece. While the watchers stood stunned and marveling, the ram rose into the air and flew away from the temple, the brother and sister clinging to his back.

But one of them was to be sacrificed to Ino's jealousy after all. The ram headed toward the coast of Asia Minor, and as he flew over the strait separating Europe from Asia, Helle fell from his back into the sea below. Ever since it has been called the Hellespont: Helle's sea. Phrixus managed to stay aboard the ram and was safely landed in the kingdom of Colchis on the eastern edge of the Black Sea. There the ram ordered the boy to kill him as a sacrifice to Zeus, which Phrixus sorrowfully did. Then the ram was skinned of its golden fleece, and the shining marvel was nailed to an oak in a sacred grove where Aeetes, the king, set a dragon to guard it. Phrixus lived on in Colchis, and when he was grown he married a daughter of Aeetes.

About this time, Aeetes received an oracle that he would rule only so long as the Golden Fleece remained in his possession. So Pelias knew full well that even if Jason should somehow manage to reach the land of Colchis, he would never be able to obtain the Golden Fleece. Aeetes would on no account give it to him. If Jason were to try to take it by force, it would prove to be all his life was worth.

START OF THE VOYAGE

None of this seemed to have entered Jason's mind as he enthusiastically began to plan for his voyage. First, of course, he would have to have a ship, such a ship as the world had never yet seen. It must be large enough to accommodate fifty rowers along with their weapons and supplies. Its planks must be made of the finest oak, held together by stout iron bolts. Jason chose a shipbuilder by the name of Argus for this important task. The ship would be called *Argo* after her builder.

Argus led his workers to the slopes of Mount Pelion

where, among the groves of oak and pine and fir, they selected the straightest among the oaks. For the fifty oars of *Argo* the best of the firs were felled. When the long planks had been sawn from the oak, they were floated in the sea's salt tides to toughen them before the bolt holes were bored.

Now one day as Argus was working on the planks that had been drawn from the water and dried, a brightness suddenly appeared beside him, and a voice spoke.

"It is the goddess Athena who now speaks to you, Argus. I have come to give you directions regarding the building of this ship, for I have Jason's adventure at heart, and *Argo* must not fail him."

"Great goddess, shining Athena, I am grateful for your help. *Argo* has challenged all I ever knew of shipbuilding," replied the astonished Argus.

"Then listen while I give you directions on how to lay her keel."

Every day thereafter, Athena directed the work on *Argo,* and one day she came with a piece of wood well worked of the finest grain of oak.

"Set this in the prow of *Argo,*" she said. "It is from one of the sacred oaks of Dodona and has the power of speech. It will help guide *Argo* through the roughest channels and warn of rocks and shoals."

Argus gladly did as she told him.

While the building of *Argo* was going on, Jason sent out word of the voyage inviting the heroes of Greece to join him in this expedition. They were quick to respond.

Jason had his pick of the greatest, and when the list of fifty-one was complete, it included such names as Heracles, Telemon, Peleus, and Orpheus.

Jason welcomed Orpheus with special gladness, though he was a musician more than he was a fighting man. He played upon a lyre and sang with such sweetness that birds flew down from their trees, and beasts came trotting from the woods and fields to listen. The very stones were often moved to tears by the sweet sadness of his singing. Orpheus had reason for sadness.

One day his bride Eurydice, while walking in her garden, was bitten on the ankle by an adder and died. Orpheus was beside himself with grief and longing, and in his great agony determined to follow his beloved to the halls of Hades and there beg for her return to Earth. Perhaps Pluto, god of the Underworld, would take pity on a grieving husband and return Eurydice to him. So taking his lyre, Orpheus bravely began the long descent to the Land of the Shades.

Charon, the ferryman who rowed doomed souls across the river Styx, which flows between the lands of the living and the dead, at first refused to take Orpheus into his boat. But when he heard the song that the young man sang for him, Charon's heart was moved to pity, and he ferried him across. Even Cerberus, the fierce three-headed dog that guards the entrance to Hades, was moved by the music to let him pass.

And now Orpheus stood within the halls of the dead

while the spirits of the dead moved like smoke around him. Before him, seated on their thrones, were Pluto and Queen Persephone. Orpheus thought he could just make out the youthful form of his dear Eurydice near the queen's throne.

Pluto fixed his visitor with a hard gaze. "How dare you, a mere mortal, enter these dread regions!"

Instead of answering the god directly, Orpheus struck his lyre and began to sing of his love for Eurydice. He sang of their happy courtship, of their wedding day, of all the hopes which the future held for them. His song was exultant and joyous like the singing of birds on a sunny morning. But then it changed. As Orpheus sang of the terrible day when Eurydice met her death, the strains which came from the lyre were so poignant with sorrow that tears began to course down the iron cheeks of Pluto, and Persephone hid her face in her hands.

At last the song ended on a broken note, and the singer stood with bowed head.

When Pluto spoke, his voice had lost its grating tone. It was almost tender and hardly above a whisper.

"And what is your wish, oh mortal?"

Orpheus raised his head. "To have Eurydice returned to me."

"So be it," declared Pluto. "What even Zeus could not do, your song has achieved. Depart now and I promise that your Eurydice will follow you. One condition I lay upon you. Do not look back until you have passed through the halls of the dead and are in the upper world."

Joy choked off the words of thanks Orpheus would have given Pluto, but the king read those words in his eyes before Orpheus quickly turned and strode back along the way he had come. He passed Cerberus, whose iron chain lay soundless on the stone floor. Charon without a word took him across the Styx, and then Orpheus began the long climb toward the upper world and the sun. He listened for the sound of Eurydice's light step behind him. He heard nothing. As he hurried upward toward the light, he tried to catch the sound of quickened breathing. Only his own footsteps rang within the tunneled passageway. Finally, as he gained the gates beyond which lay the spreading, sun-filled plain, Orpheus could bear the suspense no longer. He whirled about, and there close behind was the dear form of Eurydice in all her beauty and youthful charm. He lifted his arms to clasp her, but even as he did, she began to fade from his sight. One word escaped from her graying lips before she vanished utterly. "Farewell," she whispered, and was gone. Orpheus stood alone at the gates of Hades.

So when the word went forth that *Argo* needed stouthearted rowers, Orpheus eagerly set out for Iolcus. He needed this adventure to solace his grief and to ease the awful loneliness of his life.

At last Argus's labors were over, and *Argo* sat on the beach, her prow facing the sea. Her stout sides rose well above the sands. A wondering crowd circled her by day and night, for nothing like this ship had ever been built before, and hundreds from all over Greece had come to marvel at her. Slaves in a long, continuing line began bringing down to the ship the arms and provisions the heroes would need on their voyage. Then the heroes, too, began to file through the town, and the crowds lost interest in *Argo* as they watched these brave young men striding toward their ship.

Never before had such a noble company been gathered together. The best of Greece was here. Some of the people were dismayed that so many noble youths should be allowed to risk their lives in this adventure. But nothing could have stopped them. With eager faces and confident voices they hailed the ship, which seemed now to be straining toward the open water, as eager as they.

The moment for the launching was at hand. Logs were placed in front of *Argo* reaching from her prow to the water's edge. Heroes, slaves, and onlookers seized the ropes dangling from *Argo*'s sides, and pulling together they tipped her onto the first log, where she began to glide from that log to the next and on to the sea's edge. Smoke rose from the great oak rollers as her speed increased. She hit the water with a hissing sound and would have gone far into the harbor had the men not held her with the ropes. The cargo was put aboard, a sacrifice was made to Apollo, and then the Argonauts went aboard their ship. The long oars, twenty-five to a side, were placed in the tholes, and, with Tiphys at the helm, *Argo* with a glad cry began to move through the water. Once they were out into the harbor, the voyagers stepped the mast and raised the

sail. Caught by a fresh breeze, it filled and smoothly drove *Argo* out of the harbor and northward up the coast of Thessaly.

Orpheus played a spirited tune on his lyre to strengthen the heart of his comrades as they looked back on their vanishing homeland. The great adventure had begun.

Running before steady winds, they came after several days to the island of Lemnos. The wind failed as they approached, and they had to row *Argo* into the harbor.

This island was populated only by women. Some years before, the men of Lemnos had raided along the mainland coast and returned with women they had captured there. This so angered the women of Lemnos that they had killed their husbands and their fathers and even their sons.

When they first saw *Argo* coming into the harbor, the women of Lemnos feared it was a raiding party from the mainland, but when they discovered that the Argonauts meant them no harm, they welcomed these men. Arraying himself in the splendid robe Athena had given him, Jason went up from the ship to pay his respects to the queen, Hypsipyle.

When he reached her palace, its gates were thrown open to him, and he was led into the presence of the queen.

"Stranger," she began, "you are most welcome here. All our men have left us to work the fields in Thrace. Even our smallest sons they took with them, and now we women must forego the tasks that Athena taught us in order to plow the fields and drive the herds and work the mines. We need men to ease our tasks for us. You and your comrades are welcome to remain here as long as you wish."

So she spoke, and Jason did not know that she was lying. He thanked her for her welcome and returned to *Argo* to tell his comrades that feasting and dancing would be their reward for assisting the women of Lemnos. The Argonauts greeted this news with gladness, for they had been many days at sea and were eager for soft beds and food and wine. Even work in the fields would be a welcome relief from pulling on the oars. So they happily followed Jason back into the city. All but Heracles, who declared that he would stay by the ship with a few others whom he chose.

The days flew by in work and dance and song, and it seemed as if the Argonauts had forgotten the mission they had undertaken. The women of Lemnos had charmed them utterly. Even Jason lolled in the palace, delighting in the company of Queen Hypsipyle.

But one day Heracles strode into the city and, bellowing from the center of its square, demanded that the Argonauts gather there for a meeting. When the women came along with the men, he ordered them away.

"What I have to say is for the ears of my comrades. Away with you women," he commanded. "We have had too much of women."

Summoned by his bull's voice, Jason came from the palace.

"Ha, Jason," cried Heracles at sight of him. "A fine leader the gods have given us! Do you think the Fleece will come here of its own accord? Did we depart from

Iolcus in order to plow the fields of the ladies of Lemnos? Was *Argo* built for this purpose? We could have found brides and fields and cattle nearer home. If our captain is to spend every day basking in the smiles of Hypsipyle, the rest of us may as well go home and suffer the scorn of our people there."

As he spoke, shame stood in the eyes of the Argonauts. They hung their heads, not daring to risk a glance at Heracles's scornful face. When the meeting was over, they hurried away to gather the possessions they had taken from the ship and to make haste to return to *Argo*. With Jason leading them, they went aboard and in silence took their seats upon the rowing benches. Then with Tiphys at the helm they struck the water with their long oars and pulled away from the island of Lemnos. So they continued on their journey and made good progress, sometimes sailing before the wind and sometimes manning the oars.

One evening, just as the sun was setting, a strong wind from the south drove them into the swiftly running waters of the Hellespont. This was the roughest sea they had met with so far. High cliffs rose up on either side of *Argo*, and the waters whirling in that narrow channel broke in waves upon the surface of the sea. The faces of the men were wet with spray, and they shivered in the cold wind driving *Argo* through the strait.

The first land they came to after they passed the strait was an island known as Bear Mountain. It was inhabited by a fearful race of giants, each having six arms. But the land belonged to and was governed by the Doliones, whose king was a noble young man named Cyzicus. The king had recently married a gentle, pretty maiden called Cleite for whom he had paid a large dowry. Cleite loved her young husband, and she was the delight of his heart.

Cyzicus welcomed the Argonauts most kindly and even abandoned Cleite in order to have dinner with the strangers. Jason asked the young king many questions about this region, which was strange to him, and about the route which lay ahead. Cyzicus gave him all the information that he could.

When next morning the Argonauts attempted to leave the harbor, they found that during the night the giants had come and placed huge boulders across its mouth, penning them in. Hardly had they made this discovery, when they heard rude shouts and saw the monsters coming down the mountain toward them.

Heracles seized his bow as did the other heroes and soon their arrows had stopped the giants' charge. They lay on the beach like the long logs which had been felled for building *Argo* before those logs were sawn into planks. Side by side they lay, the dead giants, and the Argonauts left them there as a feast for birds and beasts of prey. They cleared a passage in the harbor, raised sail, and were soon speeding away from the island of the Doliones.

During all that long day they sailed, but as the sun died the wind died, too. Before they could row to shore, a mist came down upon them suddenly, followed by another wind coming from a different quarter. In an instant, the sail billowed out, and *Argo* was skimming over the water with the sea mist all about her. At last a shoreline showed before them, and they dropped the sail while *Argo*'s momentum carried her in toward the sandy beach. The Argonauts, confused by the mist and the strange shoreline, did not realize that this was the island of the Doliones, from which they had departed earlier.

It did not take long for a guard patrolling the beach to discover that a strange ship had anchored there, and quickly he gave the alarm, for raiders came frequently to these shores. Soon Cyzicus and his followers were on the beach attacking the strangers, whom in the dark and mist they failed to recognize as their new-found friends. Nor did the Argonauts recognize these attackers as their former hosts. The battle was long and bitter, and when dawn came to drive away the mist, there was great sorrowing on both sides. The young king lay dead with Jason's spear in his breast. The Argonauts joined the Doliones in bewailing the noble Cyzicus. When Cleite heard of his death, she was so overcome with grief that she hanged herself. Both were buried side by side and the Argonauts assisted at their burial.

HERACLES LOSES AN OAR

They departed from Bear Mountain in a dead calm. The sea was smooth as a pond, and *Argo* moved through the water sluggishly, propelled by her fifty oars. It almost seemed as if the ship, too, were heavy-hearted, like the heroes who manned her. The death of Cyzicus and his bride weighed sadly upon them. All that day they rowed with no breeze to lighten their labor. By day's end they were so weary that they slackened work at the oars, every man but Heracles. It seemed now that he alone was driving *Argo* forward. As the others became more exhausted, his strength seemed to grow. The force of his pulling would have sent *Argo* spinning in a circle except for the skill of Tiphys at the helm.

But the strain upon his oar proved too great at last. With a loud crack it split in two. Heracles was hurled from his bench, while the broken length was swept out of reach in the moving water.

Heracles bellowed with rage as he picked himself up, and his eyes glared around at his companions making sure none of them dared find anything amusing in his predicament. And none of the Argonauts laughed, though the sight of Heracles sprawled upon the deck was absurdly funny.

Since at all times *Argo* sailed close to shore, it did not take them long to find a good harbor in which to anchor their ship.

While the comrades began unloading supplies and searching for firewood, Heracles strode away from the shore and into the looming forest in search of a new oar. With him went Hylas, his ever-constant companion, a young lad who was dear as a son to the mighty Heracles. Hylas carried a water jar, and while the giant crashed through the undergrowth seeking a fir or pine to suit his purpose, Hylas went quietly in search of a spring.

At last Heracles found just the tree he was looking for. It rose straight and tall with few branches. The hero promptly laid down his bow and arrow, took off his lion skin, and began loosening the earth around the pine with his bronze-studded club. Then he put his shoulder against the tree and, heaving mightily, forced it out of the ground. It fell with a crash.

Off in the woods, Hylas heard that crash and smiled with satisfaction. Heracles had found a new oar. And just then Hylas found what he had been seeking. In a shady spot green with fern and violet and other shade-loving plants, and encircled with granite, a spring gushed gently forth from the base of a hill. Hylas leaned over to dip the water jar into the spring. For a moment he paused to study his reflection mirrored on the water's surface. Hylas was a handsome youth and no vainer than most youths sure of their good looks. But that moment of vanity cost him dear.

A nymph lived within the spring and when she beheld the face of Hylas, she fell in love with it. In an instant, her white arms were thrust out of the water, and she clasped Hylas around the neck. Before the lad could cry out or draw away, he was pulled down into the spring and forever lost. The water jar fallen at the edge of the spring gave mute hint of his fate.

Heracles, having trimmed the length of pine, was ready to carry it back to the ship where it could be fashioned into an oar. He balanced it on his shoulder, then called for Hylas. Only the echo of his own voice answered him. He called again. Still no answer from his dear friend.

Heracles threw off the pine log and started out in search of the youth, bellowing as he went. At last, stumbling across a small stream, he stopped to ponder the situation. It was a very small stream, he observed, and since all streams originate somewhere in a spring, Heracles decided to follow this one back to its source. Hylas had, he remembered, been looking for a spring. Kicking boulders to one side and ripping apart the underbrush that stood in his way, Heracles came at last to the fern-green glade where Hylas had found his spring. And in a moment Heracles spied the bronze water jar. So Hylas had been here. He looked eagerly around and called and called again. There was neither sight nor sound of the boy.

Now Heracles had one thought only—to find Hylas. Perhaps a wild beast had frightened him, and he had fled for his life. He was probably even now wandering about in the deeper part of the forest, trying to find his way back to the spring and Heracles. The hero seized his great club in a tighter grasp. Gone was all memory of *Argo* and her crew and the mission on which they had set themselves. The slow brain of Heracles could hold only one thought at a time. Right now that thought was all of Hylas. Crashing and cursing, the giant plunged into the darkening forest in search of him.

At first the Argonauts thought little of the giant's absence. It was not unusual for Heracles to wander off in search of game. They felt sure that with the coming of dawn they would see his huge figure emerging from the woods with Hylas, as always, in attendance.

But when the dawn did come, there was still no sign of Heracles or of Hylas, either. Now the Argonauts grew anxious. A breeze came with the day, a fair wind that Tiphys urged them to take advantage of.

"Who knows what Heracles may have decided to do?" Tiphys asked. "Perhaps he looked on the loss of his oar as an omen. It has seemed to me for some days now that Heracles was becoming weary of this adventure. Except for his battle with the giants at Bear Mountain, he has had little enough to do. Pulling at an oar day after day is hardly the kind of labor Heracles would value. It is clear to me he has gone in search of more daring occupation and taken his Hylas with him."

Some sided with Tiphys, others did not. Jason said nothing. He sat apart, his spirit broken by this disaster. It was with a high and confident heart that Jason had welcomed Heracles to the company of the Argonauts. How could their adventure go wrong with such a hero to champion it? And now Heracles was gone, and Jason's heart was heavy with foreboding.

Suddenly, as the argument over Heracles was about to come to blows, a strange figure rose out of the sea's depths. It was Glaucus speaking for the sea-god, Nereus. He clung to *Argo* while he spoke these words:

"Argonauts, listen to me well. It is folly to think you could take Heracles to Colchis. His place is in Argos, where he is fated to complete twelve great labors. Leave him to it. As for Hylas, a nymph has fallen in love with him, and you will never see him more."

With that, Glaucus let go of *Argo* and sank back into the sea.

Now the Argonauts were in good spirits again, and those who had been quarreling shook one another's hands. Their decision was made for them. If they sailed from here now before a fair wind, they would not be abandoning a comrade. His fate had been decided, and they could in no way alter it.

Only Jason sat gazing at the spot where Glaucus had disappeared. It still seemed to him that a shadow had fallen across the quest for the Golden Fleece, and in that shadow he shivered slightly.

THE JOURNEY CONTINUES

The next adventure to test the Argonauts came when they beached *Argo* in the kingdom of Amycus, a cruel, inhospitable man. He liked strange visitors no better than any other king, but instead of obeying the gods' rules for hospitality, he challenged all newcomers to a boxing match. And so great was the strength and skill of Amycus that he always managed to kill his opponent.

At the first glimpse of *Argo* upon his shore, Amycus

came striding down to stand among the Argonauts, taunting them, and challenging them to what he knew would be a fatal contest.

"Strangers," he addressed them. "No one of you may continue on your journey until you have proved yourself in a boxing match with me. Choose the best man among you for your champion and let the contest begin."

Now among the Argonauts was a young hero by the name of Polydeuces, the most famous boxer in all Greece. Therefore he stepped forward and faced Amycus.

"A few days ago when Heracles was of our company, you would not have spoken so boldly. But now my comrades have no one better than myself to represent them. I do so without fear, whoever you are. Let the fight begin."

He removed the cloak he was wearing and threw it down upon the sand. Then the fight began.

Amycus was larger than Polydeuces, but the latter was lithe and quick. And younger. Before long the confident, arrogant grin Amycus had worn as they began the match gave place to a look of ugly determination. Still he continued to rush Polydeuces, who always side-stepped lightly. The king began to tire. Polydeuces, though marked in several places by the cruel blows of Amycus, still seemed tireless. At last Amycus raised himself on tiptoe to bring down upon Polydeuces a blow that would knock him to the sands. But Polydeuces saw it coming, and cleverly took it on his shoulder, at the same time striking Amycus just behind the ear, crushing his skull. The king fell heavily and did not move again.

At the sight of this, his followers seized their spears and rushed at the Argonauts. But the heroes had expected that and were prepared. For a few moments the battle raged around the body of the dead king. But when several of his followers lay dead beside him, the others turned and fled, and the Argonauts quickly headed *Argo* out to sea in search of a more hospitable harbor.

They found one the very next day. Salmydessus happened to be the home of a very old man named Phineus. Years and years ago, Phineus had offended the gods. To punish him, Zeus had given him a long old age to live out blind. And worse: he was unable to eat because whenever a dish was put before him, winged monsters called Harpies would swoop down, snatching up whatever was on the plate and leaving a stench so awful behind them that any desire for food was lost. So Phineus was not only old and blind, but starving.

Many years before, Zeus had told Phineus that someday a body of brave Greeks that could lift the curse would visit his island. So when Phineus learned that a strange and marvelous ship, the likes of which no one had ever seen before, had anchored in the harbor, he hurried down from his house to greet the newcomers. When the Argonauts saw the shriveled form of the blind old man shuffling toward them, they marveled that one so thin and helpless could remain alive.

"Tell me from whence you come and who your leader is," Phineus said, when he had recovered breath suffi-

ciently. "If the gods are kind, then you are Greeks and my long sufferings are over."

Jason stepped forward and gently took the old man's hand. "We are indeed Greeks," he said. "I am Jason, son of Aeson, rightful king of Iolcus. We are in search of the Golden Fleece, and in my company are the greatest heroes of all time."

Phineus then told them of the terrible trials he had suffered for so long. He ended by saying, "Long ago I was given an oracle which said that the sons of Boreas, the north wind, would one day free me from the Harpies. Tell me that these two are with you now."

Among those who had joined Jason were indeed two brothers, sons of the north wind. Their names were Zetes and Calais. They were handsome youths and built like all other human beings except for wings that sprouted from their shoulder blades. This marked them as sons of Boreas. They came forward, happy to offer their services to poor, blind Phineus.

They began preparing a feast to lure the Harpies to Phineus. And sure enough, when the meat was done and placed before the starving old man, there was a rush of wings, and down from the sky came the revolting monsters. They grabbed the meat in their loathsome mouths and started away with it, leaving behind them such a stench as none there, except old Phineus, had ever smelled before.

But no sooner had the Harpies spread their wings than

the sons of Boreas were after them. Higher and higher the
pursued and pursuers climbed the sky, and though the
monsters could overtake the stormy west winds, now
the sons of the north wind were overtaking them.

Just as the two winged brothers were within reach of
the Harpies, suddenly there appeared beside them lovely
Iris, messenger of the gods.

"Sons of Boreas," she said, "you may not harm the
Harpies for they are the hounds of Zeus. But I swear to
you by the river Styx that from this day they will never
bother Phineus again."

Thus reassured, Zetes and Calais gave up the chase and
returned to their comrades and Phineus. Iris went back to
high Olympus, and the Harpies flew on to Crete, where
they hid themselves in a dark cave.

When Zetes and Calais reported what Iris had said,
there was great rejoicing, for all knew that an oath taken
on the river Styx could never be broken. Another feast was
immediately prepared which old Phineus ate most hun-
grily. Moreover, when he rose from the table, his vision
was suddenly restored to him.

"The curse upon me has been lifted," he cried. He
looked around at his companions, seeing them for the first
time. "It is you who have ended my suffering," he told
them. "Therefore demand anything of me you wish, and
if it is in my power I will grant it to you."

Jason, the leader, spoke. "Good Phineus, long-suffering
old man, we are happy that our visit here has ended your
long misery. All we ask of you is to tell us of the dangers

that lie in wait for us between this port and Colchis. And if you can, tell us how to deal with them."

Phineus was eager to tell the young men all he knew and that was a great deal. He particularly warned them about the Clashing Rocks, which came together at regular intervals in a narrow strait through which they would have to pass.

"Take a dove with you when you leave here," Phineus directed them, "and when the Clashing Rocks separate, free the dove. If it flies between them before they come together again, then *Argo* will get past when next they separate."

For several days ill winds prevented the Argonauts from leaving Phineus, and during all this time they were treated most hospitably. But at last came a dawn when the winds were favorable, and the heroes made ready to depart. They did not forget to take with them a dove to guide them past the Clashing Rocks.

And now Athena saw fit to take an active part in *Argo*'s voyage. Hardly had the great ship cleared the harbor when she came swiftly down from Olympus to await the Argonauts just where the Clashing Rocks rose above the water. Jason's adventure had been dear to her heart from the very beginning, and she would not see it ended now.

Argo approached the narrowest part of the strait, and Tiphys, the helmsman, saw the great rocks looming before them. Even as they watched, the rocks suddenly crashed together with a great swirl of water that sent spray into the air. There was a harsh, grinding sound, and the rocks separated. Tiphys instantly loosed the dove, and it darted off straight between the rocks. But just as it was almost clear, the rocks came together, and several feathers from the dove's tail fluttered down to the water.

Now it was *Argo*'s turn. As the rocks drew apart, the heroes gave a great shout and struck the water with their oars. The ship sprang forward, the dark rocks looming ahead. In perfect rhythm the oars pulled and lifted, then sliced again into the water as one. It was a race between them and the Clashing Rocks. It seemed won by the Argonauts, when a cry of despair came from the lips of Tiphys. The rocks in the opening ahead were coming together. He cried to his companions to pull harder lest they be crushed.

Then it was that Athena came into action. Bracing herself against the cliff with one hand, she placed the other against *Argo*'s stern. With a mighty shove, the goddess sent the ship forward—just as the rocks came crashing together again. Except for a few splinters lost from her stern, *Argo* was safe at last, and Athena, well pleased, returned to Olympus.

As for the Clashing Rocks, they were to remain forever after fixed to the ocean bottom, no longer a threat to voyagers.

COLCHIS

Just before reaching the city of Colchis, the Argonauts saved from the sea four young men. These were the sons of Phrixus who, as a boy, had ridden on the back of a golden ram to the land of King Aeetes. The brothers had set forth to visit their father's homeland. They had not sailed far when they were shipwrecked, and all four would have drowned if the Argonauts had not come along in time to save them.

They advised Jason not to go at once into the harbor at Colchis, but to anchor *Argo* in a marshy place among tall reeds. Jason followed their advice and while they sat hidden, he addressed his shipmates.

"My comrades," he said, "our new-found friends, the sons of Phrixus, have given me good advice. Instead of approaching the king as a body, they have advised me to take only two of you and go with them into the city of Colchis. They have offered to take us to Aeetes and to explain to their grandfather the purpose of our visit. If Aeetes refuses to give up the Golden Fleece, then we shall return to the ship, and together we can decide what seems best to do."

The Argonauts thought well of this plan, and so Jason and his comrades were put ashore at the edge of the marsh from where they proceeded on foot into the city.

The palace of Aeetes proved to be a splendid one. There were inner and outer courts with fountains playing in them. Great pillars lined colonnades onto which opened the many rooms and galleries of the palace. One large wing held the throne room and the apartments of the king and queen. Another was the residence of the two daughters of Aeetes, along with their serving maids. The elder daughter was Chalciope, the mother of Jason's new-found companions. The younger was Medea, a beautiful maiden much practiced in witchcraft.

As the men from *Argo* entered the main court, they found it full of activity. Slaves were busy cutting firewood, preparing freshly butchered meat, and performing other household chores. At the sight of the sons of Phrixus, a cry went up. These four had so recently departed their city it was most surprising to see them now. The palace had yet to learn of their shipwreck and rescue by the Argonauts.

The astonished cries of the workers and guards brought Aeetes and his queen into the courtyard. Recognizing her sons' voices, Chalciope came speeding from her chamber. For a few moments there was general consternation until it was explained that the four so recently returned had suffered shipwreck and would have been drowned had not the Argonauts come in time to save them.

Aeetes listened to the tale with a brow as black as thunder. He wanted no strangers in his country and saw in Jason a threat to him and his kingdom. Nonetheless, the strangers must first be offered hospitality.

The Argonauts were bathed and fed, and when the formalities had been taken care of, then, and only then, did Aeetes ask who they were, whence they had come, and the purpose of their visit.

Jason spoke up boldly but courteously. He explained the importance to him of taking the Golden Fleece back to Pelias. He even offered to do service for Aeetes in exchange for it.

But the wrath of Aeetes swelled as he listened to the hero. Hardly had Jason finished speaking when the king burst out, "This is all a pack of lies. It is a trick to rob me of my royal power. Get out of my country and be gone before I cut out your tongue for the lying words you have spoken."

Jason placed a hand upon his sword, but managed to keep his temper despite the insulting words.

"It is destiny which has brought me here, Aeetes," he said. "Why would I and my companions risk the dangers of unknown seas if it were not meant that we should claim the Fleece? Know, too, that we are descended from the very gods who have brought us safely here."

Jason's fearless words served somewhat to deflate Aeetes's wrath. Besides, Jason did indeed look like a descendant of gods. The king had never before seen a man as tall as this one, nor ever one with such shining golden hair. Perhaps, Aeetes thought, the gods had taken a hand in what this young man did. A crafty look settled in his eyes.

While Aeetes was thus considering Jason, another person had slipped unnoticed into the great hall where the

discussion was taking place. The princess Medea was curious to see the handsome stranger who had come from so
far away. Chalciope had reported to her sister the meeting
in the courtyard, speaking enthusiastically of the young
leader who had rescued her sons from death. So now here
was Medea contemplating Jason and seeing in him all that
Chalciope had seen. And more. As she studied him, a sudden, quick pain pierced her. She caught her breath and
pressed both hands to her breast. Had Eros, god of love,
sent an arrow into her heart? In that moment she knew as
surely as Ariadne had known when first her eyes met those
of Theseus that she, Medea, was hopelessly in love.

But unlike Theseus, Jason had eyes only for the king,
who was starting to speak again. Now his voice was calm,
almost friendly.

"If, as you claim, you are children of the gods," he said,
"then I cannot withhold the Fleece from you. But I intend
to test that claim. In a field beyond this palace are two fire-
breathing bulls with feet of bronze. Each day I yoke them
to the plow and furrow four acres of that field. Then I
sow those furrows with the teeth of a dragon slain long
ago by Cadmus, who built the city of Thebes. From this
sowing, warriors fully armed spring up. I destroy them
one by one as they come to attack me. It is morning when
I yoke the bulls and evening when the last warrior lies
dead. If you, Jason, can accomplish this task in the same
time, you may have the Golden Fleece. Otherwise it will
remain with me, the better man of us two."

Jason's heart sank as he listened. The king had set him

an impossible task. Yet honor demanded he accept the challenge even though he knew it was a trick. Aeetes had not been seen plowing this morning! For a while, Jason, musing with his eyes fixed on the stone-paved floor, considered how he should answer the king. At last he spoke, and his words rang proudly through the hall.

"Aeetes, what you intend for me and my companions is plain. Yet, had we feared death we would not be here in Colchis now. Therefore I accept your challenge, trusting in the gods who have thus far guided my quest for the Golden Fleece."

He rose from his chair, bowed to the king, and, followed by his two companions from *Argo,* left the hall.

Well before this, while *Argo* lay hidden in the reedy marsh, Athena had anticipated Jason's peril. Sharing with Hera her fears for her favorite, together they agreed that the witch-maiden, Medea, should be the means of saving him. With this plan in mind, they approached Aphrodite, mother of Eros, and persuaded her to help them. This she did by prevailing on Eros to shoot one of his magic arrows into the heart of Medea. At first sight of him, Medea was in love with Jason.

When Medea heard Jason's brave words to her father, she was filled with dismay. Was she to lose so quickly this man she loved so well? It was in her power to save him. But dared she go against her father? Would the gods forgive such a betrayal? Besides the heavy burden on her conscience, it would mean exile from her homeland—or death. Her gift of witchcraft was well known. If Jason ac-

complished his task, she would be suspected at once, and
Aeetes's anger would be murderous.

She came to her decision when Jason rose to leave the
hall. A heavy sadness settled on her. She felt she could not
bear to have him go from her sight. How then could she
face life if he were dead? Better to die with him than try
to live without him. The goddesses had schemed wisely.
A priestess of Hecate, the goddess of the Underworld,
Medea would place at Jason's service all her witch's art.

She hastened to her chambers, where she summoned
her nephew to her. Like the shipbuilder's, his name was
Argus. "Will you take a message from me to Jason?" she
asked when he appeared.

The question startled Argus, then he smiled. Despite
all her will power to prevent it, a becoming blush brightened Medea's face.

"So you intend to help him," declared Argus. "I am
glad."

"Tell him to meet me at the temple of Hecate at sunrise tomorrow."

"I will, myself, conduct him there," promised Argus,
and, taking courteous leave of his aunt, he departed.

Medea slept little that night. Long before dawn showed
above the hills, she had prepared an ointment and packed
it into a golden jar. This ointment was compounded of
many rare and magical items. Its base was a flower sprung
from the blood of tortured Prometheus when a drop fell
to earth from the talons of the departing eagle.

At the first light, Medea summoned her maidens, and

mounting her carriage drawn by two white mules, she started for the temple. As she drove through the city, people turned their faces from her, fearful of meeting her eye.

The temple rose beyond the town at the edge of a wide field. Here Medea halted her team and descended from her carriage. Surrounded by her maidens, who had flocked along behind her, she entered the temple and began the ritual singing and dancing in honor of the goddess Hecate.

Soon Jason appeared. He was alone, for Argus, sensing the special nature of this tryst, had prudently withdrawn. At the sight of the tall stranger, Medea's maidens scampered away, and she and Jason were left facing each other.

Suddenly overcome by modesty, Medea stood rooted, her eyes downcast, her face rosy with embarrassment. Jason thought he had never seen so bewitching a maiden.

"Lady," he said gently, "do not feel concern that we are here together in this holy place. I have come with the hope that you will help me. Now that I see you, that hope is strengthened. Surely your heart is as kind as you are beautiful."

What girl could resist such words? Medea raised her head. All her love for him lay in her eyes. Jason stepped forward eagerly to take her hand.

"Medea, hear me now. If you will help me in the task your father has set me, I swear that you shall have nothing to fear. When the Fleece is in my hands, I will take you back to Greece and there make you my wife. Your name will be honored everywhere as the one who saved the Argonauts from certain death. My love, born of this moment, will last into eternity."

"I will help you for the sake of that love," replied Medea. "And I will go with you back to your homeland when you have seized the Golden Fleece."

Then she showed him the jar of ointment and told him how to use it.

"Rub it well into your face and hands and all your body. It will give you great strength and confidence and protect you against the fire of the bronze-footed bulls. Drip some onto your weapons and your shield. And when you have plowed the field and sown the dragon's teeth, and the dreadful warriors have sprung from the furrows, then throw a heavy rock among them. They will start to quarrel with one another, and you must spring among them wielding your sword. So you will smite them and kill them every one. By nightfall your task will be accomplished."

Jason took tender leave of Medea and hurried back to where his comrades awaited the outcome of the tryst. The Argonauts were overjoyed to hear that Jason was to have Medea's help. And they were quite willing that the princess should go with them when the time came to quit Colchis.

Next morning they all accompanied their leader when he went to meet the king. Aeetes handed Jason the dragon seeds saved from Cadmus's sowing and later given him by Athena. Jason had, of course, spread the magic ointment over his body and on his shield and weapons. It made him feel a strength equal to the gods'.

Jason had just time to drop the dragon's teeth into his helmet when he heard the pounding of brazen feet. Out of a nearby cave the two fire-breathing bulls bore down upon him. Heartened and protected by Medea's magic, Jason stood confidently awaiting them. When the first came within reach, he took hold of its horns and wrestled it to its knees. He quickly yoked it to the waiting plow, then whirled to deal with the second. The watching Argonauts trembled with fear for their leader as the flames from the monsters' nostrils enveloped him. But Medea's magic ointment was keeping Jason safe. Soon they saw him snub the plow into the ground and start the first furrow.

Now that they had met their master, the bulls were entirely subdued. Heads down and moving steadily, they might have been barnyard beasts except for the fire still flowing from their nostrils and the light glinting off their brazen feet. Jason dropped the dragon's teeth behind him in each furrow as he went. The day wore on, and the field became dotted with the forms of warriors growing gradually out of the soil.

At last all four acres were plowed, and the armed men stood along the furrows. Now Jason took up a huge boulder lying at the edge of the field. Bracing his legs, he lifted it high above his head and flung it toward the field-born warriors. Instantly they fell upon each other with fierce

shouts and the clang of deadly weapons. Jason drew his
sword and sprang among them as Medea had directed.
Hour after hour the battle raged, and one by one the warriors fell. When the sun went down, Jason stood alone
upon the field, the warriors dead around him. His task
was done.

He turned wearily to where Aeetes and his court had
grouped themselves to watch his labors, half expecting to
see the king come toward him with the Golden Fleece.
But Aeetes was already hurrying back to his palace, more
than ever determined to be rid of Jason and his comrades.

That night was another sleepless one for Medea. She
knew her father sat in his throne room surrounded by the
men of his court plotting how next to be rid of the Argonauts. She felt sure, too, that he already suspected her part
in Jason's success. Her maidens had certainly seen her
talking with him in the temple. Perhaps one of them had
reported the meeting. She, no less than Jason, was in great
peril. Her only hope lay in escape.

Grieving, she took leave of all her possessions and cut
off a length of her hair and placed it on her bed as a re-
membrance for her mother. Well she knew she would
never see this girlhood home again. Then, drawing a veil
over her head, she ran barefoot through the palace, across
the great courtyard, and away beyond the city walls to
where she knew *Argo* lay at anchor.

The moon shone down upon her as she fled, lighting
her way to the river where she could see the campfire of
the Argonauts. Standing on the high bank, she called

three times across the water, and three times she was answered by one of the sons of Phrixus who, with Jason, recognized her voice. At once, the Argonauts sprang into their ship and rowed across the river to meet her. Jason leaped ashore ahead of all the others. He was followed quickly by Phrontis and Argus, two of the sons of Phrixus.

"Save me and save yourselves," Medea cried as soon as they had joined her. "Aeetes knows all and soon will be in pursuit of us. Let us go before he can mount his chariot."

"But what of the Fleece?" cried Jason.

"I will help you obtain the Fleece," promised Medea. "But you, Jason, must vow here in the presence of your comrades to make good your promise to take me back with you to Greece, there to make me your wife. Do not let me face disgrace in a land far from home."

She fell at his feet weeping, and he raised her tenderly and drew her close. "Medea, I owe you my life and I here swear by that life you saved to keep you and honor you always as my dear wife."

She drew away from him and turned quickly toward the ship. "I will take you to the sacred grove where the Fleece hangs on the great oak. Only let us make haste."

Jason handed her aboard and the men took their places on the rowing benches. In another moment, *Argo* was moving smoothly through the moonlit water.

They reached the sacred grove just before dawn. Medea told them where to stop, then she and Jason went ashore alone.

As they went forward under the trees, suddenly a loud hissing filled the night. The serpent which guarded the Fleece was aware of their approach. He lifted his long neck and extended it toward them. Jason halted, horrified by the sight of the hideous monster. But Medea went bravely on until she stood under the slavering jaws. All the while she softly crooned an incantation that seemed to soothe the huge snake. His coils relaxed, and slowly his head lowered until the great jaws were flat upon the ground. Next she sprinkled his eyes with a drug from a small vial, which she had concealed in her bodice. The dragon's eyes closed, and all his long length reaching back into the grove became inert and lifeless.

Medea called to Jason. As from a trance he sprang forward and seized the Golden Fleece, which hung gleaming like a sunrise in the giant oak. Quickly he lowered it, and, as the shining wonder enveloped him, his heart leaped at the thought of the precious weight upon him. Here at last, hanging from his shoulder to the ground, was the treasure he had come so far to seek. Here at last was the Golden Fleece! The thought suddenly struck him that some god or mortal might come upon them and seize the Fleece, and so Jason cut short his admiration. He rolled up the treasure and hurried with Medea back to the ship.

The dawn was breaking now. But before they could be persuaded to depart, each Argonaut had to feel the Fleece and marvel at its shimmering beauty. They, too, had come through perils for this moment, and no threat of danger could keep them from fingering the treasure and feasting their eyes on it. At last Jason rolled it up again and covered it carefully. The Argonauts fell to their oars, and in the strengthening light *Argo* began her escape from Colchis, the Golden Fleece safely aboard.

HOMEWARD BOUND

By the time Aeetes had gathered his forces and mounted into his chariot, *Argo* had cleared the mouth of the river, and was standing out to sea.

In a rage the king addressed his captains, threatening them all with destruction if they failed to return the Fleece and Medea to him. His blood cried for revenge against the daughter who had betrayed him.

The Colchians quickly launched their ships and started in pursuit of Jason. Like sea birds that at sundown quit their feeding grounds and fly low above the water toward their bedding rocks in unbroken lines from headland to headland, so the ships of Aeetes sped toward the river mouth and the open sea.

The Argonauts quickly held a counsel. They decided not to return home by the way they had come, but to leave the Black Sea by way of the Ister, known today as the Danube. One half of the Colchian force was fooled by this maneuver. But the other half, led by Medea's brother Apsyrtus, suspecting Jason's plan, headed their ships for

the Ister. He doubled a neck of land and entered the river
mouth ahead of *Argo,* whose crew, unfamiliar with these
waters, had sailed the length of the triangular island at
the river mouth. There were many small islands dotting
the water all about, and the Argonauts were confused as
to where the estuary lay. Outnumbered as they were, they
thus found themselves in a hazardous position. Again they
held a counsel.

After much argument it was decided that, since Aeetes
had promised Jason the Golden Fleece, they should keep
it. But Medea, they decided, they would put ashore on one
of the islands where a temple to Artemis stood. There she
would await the judgment of some disinterested king who
would be consulted on what her fate should be. It seemed
to them a reasonable proposition to put to Apsyrtus in
exchange for a truce. Medea, however, took a sharply different view.

When she learned of the plan, outrage seized her. Sum-
moning Jason to a spot away from his comrades, she
loosed on him the full blast of her fury.

"So this is how you repay the sacrifice I have made for
you!" she said in a voice shaking with anger. "This is my
reward for saving you from the bulls and for delivering
the Fleece into your hands! The humblest slave in my
father's palace has more honor than you. Do you think any
king, however disinterested in my quarrel with my father,
will judge in favor of me? Of course he will decree that I
must return to Colchis, there to face the wrath of Aeetes.
This king-judge may himself one day have a daughter who

will betray him. I am doomed at the hands of such a judge."

A strange light had come into her eyes and fear stood in Jason's.

"Listen well, Jason, and remember these words. If you break your oath to me, you will live to regret it, for you will have Medea's curse upon you."

The words were ominous and so was the expression on the face of this beautiful witch. Jason decided to placate her.

"Medea," he began, "how can you hold such bitter thoughts toward me? I have only tried to gain time to work out of our dangerous position. We can't do battle. The Colchian horde would make quick work of our small number. And don't think Apsyrtus would show you any mercy once I am dead. He would drag you back to Colchis like a helpless slave girl to face your father. I have no wish to abandon you; I only seek some way to give you a chance to escape along with us."

His words had the desired effect upon his lovely listener. Calmly she answered him.

"I saved you by treachery. Now treachery must save you again. Arrange your truce with Apsyrtus, then lure him to the island of Artemis where you planned to leave me. He must come unarmed. But before he comes, you will hide yourself there. I will await my brother with gifts, and, while I plead with him to let you and the Argonauts go and me with you, then you must come swiftly from your hiding place and kill him."

Jason, desperate as he was, sickened as he listened to her scheme. How could he bring himself to cut down an unarmed man, one who had put his trust in him? Was there no end to Medea's wiliness? Still, Jason reasoned, he had no love for Apsyrtus, and if their positions were reversed he had no doubt the Colchian would behave no more honorably. And, too, Jason felt more responsible for his comrades' safety than for his own honor. With Apsyrtus dead, it was unlikely that the Colchians would have any interest in further pursuit of the Argonauts. They would be free at last to sail home to Iolcus. He would accept Medea's plan, hateful though it was to him.

They had no difficulty in persuading Apsyrtus to come unarmed to the little island where the temple to Artemis stood. Watching from behind a screen of bushes, Jason saw Medea take her brother's hand in friendship and lead him up the beach and away from the boat and the rowers who had brought him to her. When she had come near to the place where Jason lay in wait, she began talking most earnestly with pitiful, pleading eyes. All the while, she was skillfully maneuvering Apsyrtus into a position where his back was turned to the spot where Jason huddled with drawn sword. Then Medea gave the signal and Jason bounded forth, his naked sword held high. Apsyrtus had no time to cry out before his assailant brought the sword down upon his unhelmeted head, splitting his skull in two.

Jason immediately set about burying the dead body while Medea held a flaming torch high as a signal for the

Argonauts to approach the island. Soon *Argo* was beached
beside the boat which had brought Apsyrtus. The two
Colchian boatmen were quickly killed. Then the Argonauts scrambled up the beach where Medea and Jason
quietly awaited them.

During the counsel which followed, it was decided the
Argonauts should row away under cover of the darkness
and before the Colchians could learn of the murder of
their leader. And so it was done. Even as Jason had suspected, the Colchians had no interest in further pursuit
of the Greeks. Nor did they have any wish to return to
Colchis since both the Fleece and Medea had escaped
them. And Apsyrtus was dead. They chose instead to
settle among the people inhabiting the islands at the great
river's mouth.

As for the Argonauts, they sailed safely home, en-
countering many adventures on the way. Jason married
Medea as he had promised to do and had his revenge on
Pelias, who was killed through another of Medea's
treacheries. It was a dubious triumph, though, for Jason
and his witch-wife were exiled from Iolcus as a result, so
Jason never came into his kingdom. He and Medea went
to live in Corinth. There she bore him two sons, whom
she later murdered when Jason betrayed her.

Legend does not tell us what finally became of the
Golden Fleece. But the good ship *Argo* endures forever
as a constellation in the starry heavens.

Arachne

The family of Immortals dwelling on Mount Olympus was jealous of its power. Sometimes they were jealous of one another, and as in most families there were often quarrels among them. But they were united in their intolerance of any mortal who dared defy them. Such arrogance the Greeks called *hubris,* which was always punished swiftly by Nemesis, the goddess of retribution. We still use both words in our speech today. By hubris we mean not defiance of the gods but an insolent pride. Nemesis is the punishment which follows on the trail of anyone who considers himself invincible.

The story of Arachne is the story of a girl who dared defy Athena, and who suffered nemesis as a result.

Arachne was a country maiden who was famous throughout the land for her skill at weaving. No person on Earth, it was said, could weave so skillfully as she. There were some who said that not even Athena, goddess of all household arts, could weave so well as Arachne.

Among these arrogant boasters was Arachne herself, who was not at all modest about her skill. She never bothered to consider it a gift of the gods, nor was she ever humbly grateful for it. Instead, she was foolishly proud of it and even made fun of the work of girls less gifted than she. But then, one had to admit it was a wondrous sight to see her fingers moving lightly and swiftly back and forth across her loom. Her designs were intricate and beautiful, and she wove the colors of her threads with the ease and smoothness of an artist working with brush and paint. So graceful was she in all her motions that often the wood nymphs left their shadowy hiding places to watch her at work.

In time Arachne's fame and her boasting reached the ears of Athena, and the goddess decided to draw the girl into a contest that would cure her arrogant pride.

One day, when Arachne was weaving in a pleasant grove, there suddenly appeared beside her a bent old woman. She gazed for a moment at Arachne's loom and then said, "That is a pretty piece of weaving, my dear, and yet I have seen the time in my youth when I could have done as well."

At this Arachne threw up her head and said in a scornful tone, "Never did any mortal weave as I am weaving now, old woman."

"Those are rash words," said the old woman, and a

strange angry light came into her gray eyes, which were exceedingly youthful for one so bent with years. "It is foolish to take too great pride in what one can do, for surely there is always someone who can do the task even better."

"Not so," cried the angry girl. "There is no one who can weave better than I."

The old woman smiled and shook her head doubtfully. "Allowing that no mortal can weave as well as you, at least among the Immortals there is one who can surpass you in the art."

Arachne left off her weaving to stare at the old woman. "And who is that, pray?"

"The goddess Athena," replied the old woman.

Arachne laughed scornfully. "Not even Athena can weave as well as I."

At these words, the wood nymphs who had come to watch Arachne began to whisper among themselves. They were frightened, for it was dangerous for any mortal to set himself above the gods in anything. Foolish Arachne!

On hearing the boastful words, the old woman's eyes again flashed angrily. But in a moment they softened, and she said, "You are young and have spoken foolishly and in haste. Surely you did not mean what you said. I will give you a chance to take back your words."

But Arachne flung up her head defiantly. "I did mean what I said, and I shall prove it."

"Prove it then," cried the old woman in a terrible voice. A cry went up from the encircling crowd, and Arachne's face turned white as a cloud bank. For the old woman had vanished, and in her place stood the shining form of the goddess Athena.

"For long," she said, "I have heard your boasting and have watched your growing vanity. Now it has led you to defy the very gods. It is time you received a lesson from which other mortals as foolish and vain as you may profit. Let the contest begin."

Another loom was set up in the pleasant grove, and Arachne and the goddess began to weave. News of the contest spread through the quiet meadow and up the mountain heights. Soon a large crowd of shepherds drew near to watch the weavers.

Athena wove upon her loom a bright tapestry that told the story of other foolish mortals who had thought themselves greater than the gods, and who had been punished for their pride. Arachne pictured on her loom the stories which told of the foolish acts of the gods.

The colors used by the two weavers were so bright they might have been plucked from the rainbow. The weaving was so perfect that the figures on each loom seemed to be alive and breathing. The watchers marveled that such skill could be on Earth or in heaven.

At last the tapestries were finished, and the two contestants stood back to see what each had wrought upon her loom. Athena was so angered by what the girl had dared to picture in her work that she struck the tapestry with her shuttle, splitting the cloth in two. Then she struck Arachne on the forehead. Immediately there swept over the girl a deep remorse at her vanity in setting herself above the very gods. So great was her shame that she went at once and hanged herself. But when Athena beheld her lifeless body, she took pity upon the foolish Arachne.

"Live," she said, "but never must you be allowed to forget the lesson you have learned today. Though you may live, you must hang throughout all eternity—you and all who come after you and are of your flesh and blood."

With that, she sprinkled Arachne with bitter juices, and at once Arachne's hair and ears and nose disappeared. Her whole body shrank. Her head grew small, and she took the shape of a spider. And to this day, from her body she draws the thread with which she spins her web. And to this day, often we come upon her hanging by that thread, just as Athena said she must hang throughout all eternity.

GLOSSARY

Acrisius   a krĭs'ĭ ŭs

Aeson   ē'son

Aeetes   ē ē'tēz

Agenor   a jē'nor

Aglauros   a glaw'ros

Alcyoneus   al sĭ'o nus

Amazons   ăm'a zŏnz

Amycus   ăm'ĭ kus

Andromeda   an drŏm'ĕ da

Anteia   an ti' a

Aphrodite   ăf rŏ dī'tē

Apsyrtus   ap ser'tŭs

Arachne   a răk'nē

Arcadia   ar kā'dĭ ă

Ares   ā'rēs

Argo   ar'gō

Argonauts   ar'gō nawts

Argos   ar'gŏs

Argus   ar'gŭs

Ariadne   ar ĭ ăd'nē

Artemis   ar'tĕ mĭs

Athamas   ăth'a măs

Athena   a thē'na

Atlas   ăt'lăs

Bellerophon   be ler'ŏ fŏn

Boreas   bō'rĕ ăs

Cadmus   kăd'mŭs

Calais   kăl'a ĭs

Cassiopea   kas'ĭ o pē'a

Cecrops   sē'krŏps

Cepheus   sē'fūs

Chalciope   kel sĭ'o pē

Charon   kā'rŏn

Chimaera   kī mē'ra

Cleite   klī'tē

Colchian   kŏl'ki an

Colchis   kŏl'kĭs

Corinth   kŏr'ĭnth

Cronus   krō'nŭs

Cyzicus   sīz'ĭ kus

Danae   dăn'a ē
Dictys   dĭk'tĭs
Dodona   dō dō'na
Doliones   do li ō'nēz

Enceladus   ĕn sel'a dŭs
Envy   ĕn'vĭ
Eos   ē'ŏs
Eros   ē'ros
Ethiopia   ē thĭ ō'pĭ a
Eurydice   ū rid'ĭ sē

Glaucas   glaw' kŭs
Gorgon   gawr'gŭn

Hades   hā'dēz
Harpies   har'pĭz
Hecate   hĕk'a tē
Helicon   hĕl'ĭ kŏn
Helle   hĕl'lē
Hellespont   hĕl'ĕs pŏnt
Hephaestus   he fĕs'tŭs
Heracles   her'a klēz
Hermes   hŭr'mēz
Herse   hur'sē
Hesperides   hĕs pĕr'ĭ dēz
Hippocrene   hip'o krēn
Hylas   hĭ'lăs
Hyperboreans
   hī per bō're anz
Hypsipyle   hĭp sĭp'ĭ lē

Ino   ī'nō
Io   ī'ō
Iobates   ī ob'a tēz
Iolcus   ĭ ol'kus
Iris   ī'rĭs
Ister   is'ter

Jason   jā' sŭn

Larissa   la ris'a
Lemnos   lem'nos
Lycia   lish'i a
Lydia   lĭd'i a

Medea   me dē'a
Medusa   mē dŭ'sa
Minotaur   mĭn'ō tor

Nemesis   nĕm'e sĭs
Nereus   nē'rūs

Olympus   ō lĭm'pŭs
Orpheus   or'fē ŭs
Ossa   ŏs'a

Pallas   păl'as
Pandora   păn dō'ra
Pegasus   pĕg'a sŭs
Peleus   pē'lūs
Pelias   pē'lĭ ăs
Pelion   pē'lĭ ŏn
Persephone   pĕr sĕf'ō nē

Perses   per'sēz
Perseus   pur'sūs
Philonoe   fil ō nō'ē
Phineus   fin'ē ūs
Phlegra   fleg'ra
Phrixus   frĭk'sŭs
Phrontis   fron'tis
Pirene   pī rē'nē
Pluto   Plōō'tō
Polydectes   pŏl ĭ dek'tēz
Polydeuces   pŏl ĭ dū'sēz
Polyidus   pŏl ĭ ī'dus
Poseidon   pō sī' dŏn
Proetus   prō ē'tŭs
Prometheus   prō mē'thūs

Salmydessus   sal mi des us
Solymi   sol'i mē
Styx   stĭks

Telemon   tel'a mon
Thebes   thēbz
Theseus   thē'sūs
Thessaly   thĕs'a li
Tiphys   tī'fis
Thrace   thrās
Tiryns   tī'rinz
Titan   tī'tăn

Zetes   zē'tēz
Zeus   zūs

ABOUT THE AUTHOR

DORIS GATES was born and grew up in California, not far from Carmel, where she now makes her home. She was for many years head of the Children's Department of the Fresno County Free Library in Fresno, California. Their new children's room, which was dedicated in 1969, is called the Doris Gates Room in her honor. It was at this library that she became well known as a storyteller, an activity she has continued through the years. The Greek myths—the fabulous tales of gods and heroes, of bravery and honor, of meanness and revenge—have always been among her favorite stories to tell.

After the publication of several of her books, Doris Gates gave up her library career to devote full time to writing books for children. Her many well-known books include *A Morgan for Melinda* and the Newbery Honor Book, *Blue Willow*.